Practice Makes Perfect

by

Caroline Anderson

Dales Large Print Books
Long Preston, North Yorkshire,
England.

British Library Cataloguing in Publication Data.

Anderson, Caroline
   Practice makes perfect.

A catalogue record for this book is
available from the British Library

ISBN 1-85389-805-8 pbk

First published in Great Britain by Mills & Boon Ltd., 1991

Published in Large Print 1998 by arrangement with Harlequin
Books S.A.

Dales Large Print is an imprint of
Library Magna Books Ltd.
Printed and bound in Great Britain by
T.J. International Ltd., Cornwall, PL28 8RW.

For my mother,
who was always there for me.
Bless you

CHAPTER ONE

As the taxi-driver stacked the last of her cases on the step Lydia gave him a weary smile and an excessively generous tip, and then watched him out of sight.

Then, and only then, did she allow her gaze to wander lovingly over the familiar contours of the warm red-brick Georgian house.

Home.

She thought she had never been so glad to be back. In the raw wetness of a blustery February afternoon, after a horrendous flight from Calcutta with a long unscheduled stop in Zurich for emergency engine repairs, Lydia felt the icy blast of the wind clean through to her bones, and welcomed it.

A hot bath and a long sleep were definitely what the doctor ordered, she thought with a wry grin, and, slipping her key into the lock, she turned it and leant against the door. Nothing happened. With a slight frown she tried the key again and heard the lock turn, but still the door held firm.

'Funny,' she muttered. 'It must be bolted. Wonder why?'

Abandoning her luggage, she went round the side of the big house and made her way to the kitchen door, casting a critical eye over the garden as she went. What she saw made her frown again, but a sudden slashing downpour worthy of April dragged her attention from the overrun herbaceous border to the more immediate problem of finding a way in—and fast!

Once again, though, she found herself thwarted, and, shivering down into the inadequate layers of her ancient mac, she glared at the door and worked her way back to the front door again, ignoring the plants that thrashed her legs with drenching regularity.

What was going on?

The surgery was in darkness, and peering in through the windows told her nothing—nothing, that was, that she didn't already know, in other words, Gramps was nowhere to be seen, there was nobody manning the surgery and she was getting wetter by the minute.

One last hope remained, and, tackling

the sodden borders again, she struggled round to the other side and rattled the door of the conservatory.

Joy! It creaked open, and then slammed shut with a crash as a gust of wind caught it and snatched it out of her hand.

Breaking the sudden silence that followed, the sound of the rain pelting down on to the glass roof and gurgling in the gutters only served to soothe away the feeling of uncertainty that Lydia experienced.

The wicker rocker was where she had expected to find it, a little damp because of the time of year but still offering comfort to the travel-weary. Snuggling into its lumpy old cushions, she let her eyes drift shut and settled down to wait for Gramps.

Sam gathered up his bag, slammed the car door and made a run for the house, letting himself in by the side-door. He shed his trench coat on the way up to his flat, and hung it over the bath to drip while he filled the kettle and hunted in the fridge for something quick and easy to eat before evening surgery.

While the kettle boiled he munched on a cold tandoori chicken leg and replayed

9

the messages on his answer-phone.

Mrs Jacobs was wondering if he could fit her in tonight because her waterworks were giving her trouble again and she didn't think she should wait until Monday; Judith, the district nurse, had flu and would be off for the next few days; the village shop had his order ready and could he go down and collect it before five-thirty—answer: no, because it was now ten past and he had evening surgery in twenty minutes; and young David Leeming had cut his hand and his mother didn't know if it needed stitching and should she take him along to the hospital or would Dr Davenport be able to deal with it? Dr Davenport never did find out what she had decided, because she was still procrastinating when the tape ran out.

He rang Judith, told her to stay in bed, drink plenty and take paracetomol QDS, which got him a flea in his ear for waking her up to tell her something so obvious. He apologised meekly, promised to call in the morning and hung up, a frown creasing his brow.

With the practice running at full stretch, half the village in the grip of a vile flu bug and the other half falling over on the slush

10

and sustaining fractures, sprains and other less serious injuries in addition to the usual work-load, the very last thing Sam needed was Judith out of the running.

He went into the bathroom, changed places with his mac and showered briskly, towelling himself roughly dry in the kitchen as he made a coffee and rummaged in the fridge again. Coming up with a yoghurt two weeks past its sell-by date, the curled remains of a quiche and a flaccid lettuce, he opted for safety and put the last two bits of bread into the toaster, hung up the towel and dressed quickly.

Unfortunately the toast got stuck. Cursing fluently and sucking his burned fingertips, he opened the window and chucked the burnt offerings out into the rain-swept night, and slammed the window back down unnecessarily hard. It had probably been mouldy, anyway, he thought with weary resignation.

The phone rang—Mrs Leeming had decided that Dr Davenport should be given the dubious privilege of sewing up young David, and she would be bringing him in to the surgery. Would that be all right?

'Fine. I'll see when I can fit you in,' he

11

said a trifle abruptly, and hung up, eyes scanning the kitchen for anything else to eat. He really should have remembered about the village shop. There was nothing fit for human consumption in the entire place—in fact, he doubted that the mice would bother with half of what was left. He hoped it wasn't an omen—it was his weekend on call.

Giving food up as a bad job, he downed his coffee, made another one and took it downstairs with him.

As usual, going into the consulting-room restored his sense of balance, and he sat in the old leather chair, propped his feet on the edge of Harry Moore's desk and sighed contentedly.

He had never meant to be a country GP. Hospital medicine—probably cardiology, or neurology, or one of the other prestigious branches—had beckoned, until a chance comment by his father one day had prompted him to investigate the possibilities.

They had been arguing, as usual, about the benefits of education and informed opinion, and his father, one of the old school, who felt that the patient should be kept as ignorant as was humanly possible of the workings of his own body, had turned to Sam with a disgusted snort and told him that the next thing would be that he'd be going into general practice.

Sam had smiled grimly, congratulated his father on an accurate character assessment for once in his life, and stormed out of the prestigious Harley Street consulting-rooms with his pride intact and the seeds of revenge burning in his mind.

By the following day the anger had gone, but the idea remained, and Sam had found, at last, what he had been looking for.

That had been five years before, and now, thanks in part to his father and thanks also to Harry Moore, an old-timer from the other side of the coin, he was here, a country doctor in the best tradition of Richard Gordon, with nearly two and a half thousand patients all dependent on him for their health and welfare. It was a huge practice for one man, covering two villages and their outlying farms, and Harry had talked originally of taking Sam on as a junior partner when he recovered from his illness, but the best-laid plans and all that...

Sam knew it would make sense to take

on another partner—had even made noises on the subject to George Hastings, another one-man outfit three miles away, with whom he had set up an on-call rota—but his previous experience had made him very wary. Working alone was best, for him at least, for as long as he could manage it. When he couldn't—well then, there would be time to think again.

Sam broke from his reverie and went out into the waiting-room to greet the first of the patients.

Almost two hours and fifteen patients later, he locked up the surgery and dispensary, ran upstairs for a warm, dry coat and let himself out into the night.

The rain had stopped a short while before, but the trees were dripping steadily and he turned up his coat collar and shrugged down into its depths. At least the rain had washed away the last of the slush.

His breath misting on the cold air, he headed off down the main street towards the pub, where he bought a portion of hot stew and a jacket potato to take away, declining the offer of a swift half with the old boys in the corner. He really was too tired tonight to do anything but crawl home and go to bed.

As he turned back into the drive he noticed the luggage stacked neatly in the front porch by the main door. Frowning, he crossed the gravel and flicked his torch curiously over the battered cases.

A luggage label caught his eye; juggling the stew, he flipped the label and scanned it with the torch.

'Dr Lydia Moore.'

That meant only one thing to Sam—trouble, with a capital T.

Sighing heavily, he let himself back in, put the cases in the surgery, stashed the stew and potato in the oven, turned it on low and set about finding the missing woman.

When he had checked all the downstairs rooms he shone the torch through the glass door that led to the conservatory, and blinked in surprise. Snuggled up on Harry's favourite old chair, with her long dark hair falling like spun silk across her face, was a tall, slender girl, her tanned legs curled up under her, her hand tucked beneath the soft curve of her cheek like a child. Her lashes lay like black crescents against her fine cheekbones, emphasising the delicate structure of her face, and where her coat had fallen open he could see the soft thrust of her breast against the thin fabric of her blouse.

As he watched she shivered and shifted slightly in the chair, murmuring in her sleep.

Squashing the sudden protective urge that arose in him, Sam pushed open the door and ruthlessly shone the torch in her eyes.

Lydia was woken by a fierce light against her eyelids. Blinking and turning her head away, she straightened her stiff neck and sat up slowly, trying to see beyond the beam of light to the person holding the torch.

'Gramps?' she murmured.

The torch-bearer lowered the light so that it formed a pool around his feet. She knew he was a man because of the tan leather brogues and the soft greeny-grey of the fine wool trousers, but other than that she could tell nothing—not his height, hair colour, age—nothing.

However, she didn't think a rapist would be likely to wear brogues, so she rose to her feet, straightened her clothes and held out her hand.

'I'm Lydia Moore—'

'I know,' he said brusquely, and turned away. 'You'd better come in.'

He led her through the dining-room, out into the hall and through the door at the end into the practice premises.

There he switched off his torch and turned, and she got her first look at this stranger in her grandfather's house.

He was fairly tall, perhaps six feet, well-built but not heavy, and his thick hair was the colour of polished chestnuts, short and well cut, but rumpled as if he had run his hands through it. One heavy lock had escaped and fallen forward over his eyes, and as she watched he thrust it back with impatient fingers and she was able to see his face clearly.

His mouth was drawn into a tight line, his full lips compressed with...anger? And the hazel eyes, which she guessed were more usually softened with sympathy and humour, were glittering with irritation and—yes, it was anger, and, unless she was mistaken, directed at her.

'May I ask who you are and why you're here?' she enquired coolly, and he gave a short, humourless laugh.

'Didn't your grandfather tell you?'

17

Realisation came with a flash. 'You're the locum,' she said stupidly, and added, 'I'm sorry, I should have realised, but it's been a horrendous flight and I was exhausted. Of course, Gramps has talked about you. I hope I didn't startle you, turning up like this without any warning.'

'Oh, I knew you were coming,' he said enigmatically, and his voice was tinged with bitterness. 'As for why I'm here, someone had to be, and you were too busy chasing rainbows and playing God to do your duty by a feeble old man—'

'Feeble? Gramps? Don't be ridiculous! There never was such a tough old bird—'

'Once, maybe, but not recently. Recently he needed you, but where were you? Gadding about in some God-forsaken little mission hospital, saving souls when you should have been here by his side, holding his hand, washing him, changing his sheets, sitting with him through the long hours of the night when the pain became too much, but no, you had to play God in your paddy fields with the natives and let him rot here all alone! Charity begins at home, Lydia—didn't anyone ever tell you that?' His voice was shaking with anger, all the more

18

forceful for being held so firmly in check.

'I'm here now,' she said furiously, stung by his attitude and shocked by his words, 'and I'll thank you to mind your own business!'

'It is my business!' he shouted, his iron control slipping. 'When there's no one else here that makes it my business! I was here when he needed me—and where the hell were you?'

She drew herself up, and looked him in the eye. 'Playing God—you've said so yourself, at least twice. Well, thank you for your help. I'll take over now. I'm back for good, so I can run the practice—'

'Over my dead body will you run my practice!'

They glared at each other across the waiting-room, and slowly his words sank in.

'*Your* practice? Since when has it been *your* practice?'

He let out his breath on a long sigh. 'Since December. Didn't your grandfather tell you?'

She shook her head. 'No. No, he always calls you the locum. Well, recently he's called you Sam, but he never said anything

19

about your taking over the practice.'

Sam gave a snort of derision. 'I don't suppose he thought you'd be interested. After all, you were out there in India with your lover—'

'He wasn't my lover!' she protested, almost amused by the preposterous suggestion.

'No? What's the matter, wasn't he taken in by the innocent-little-girl act?'

Lydia thought of Jim Holden, the doctor whom she had gone to India to help, and she could barely suppress a smile. In his late fifties, widowed for ten years, he was a gentle father-figure, and when he had come back from his leave with the lovely, sweet-natured Anne as his wife Lydia had been only too pleased for him—pleased, and relieved, because Anne was a doctor and so Lydia was superfluous and could terminate her contract three months early and come home to Gramps—because, reading between the lines, all was not well and he needed her. But Jim? She let the smile show.

'On the contrary, he took it very seriously. He was very protective towards me—not to mention unfailingly polite!'

Sam gave a nasty little smile. 'You'll

forgive me if I'm not so polite, but, you see, I happen to find your sort particularly odious. Still, I suppose I should be thankful for small mercies. At least you didn't make the mistake of turning up in time for the funeral and feigning distress.'

Lydia all but stamped her foot. 'How dare you? I'll have you know that, when my grandfather dies, not only will I be at his funeral, but my "distress" will be totally genuine!'

'Very touching, but a trifle misplaced. The funeral was last week. I'm afraid you've missed your chance to put on this devastating display of genuine emotion, but never mind. At least you've got the house. I imagine that's what you wanted? Oh, and the practice, but I'm afraid you can't have that. It's mine, and, furthermore, so are the premises. He willed them to me. You can contest it, of course, but I doubt if it will get you anywhere.'

He had turned away, straightening a stack of magazines on the table in the corner with an angry thump, and so he failed to see the colour drain slowly from her face. As the meaning of his words penetrated through the fog of her tiredness and confusion she felt shock like cold hands race over her skin, and she started to tremble.

'What?' she tried to say, but her voice deserted her and all she managed was a croak.

He turned back to her, a savage retort on his lips, but it died a death as he saw her face, pale with shock, and her wide, sightless eyes that tried to focus on him. 'Oh, my God,' he murmured, 'you mean you really didn't know?'

At his words she gave a little whimper of distress, and with a startled exclamation he crossed to her and caught her against his chest as her legs buckled.

Her eyelids fluttered closed, and he could see her lips moving, forming the word 'no', over and over again. Cursing himself fluently, he scooped her up into his arms and carried her up to his flat, putting her down gently on the sofa.

About the only palatable thing left in the house was the brandy, and he poured both of them a stiff measure and pressed a glass into her hand, curling her stiff fingers around the bowl and urging it to her lips.

She coughed and tried to lower the glass, but he made her take another sip, and then took it from her and placed it on the table within reach. Picking up his own, he downed a hearty gulp and then set it down on the table with hers.

Finally he met her eyes, and the pain he saw there made him doubt all his preconceived ideas about her being a cold-hearted, gold-digging little bitch. She looked lost, afraid, and absolutely desolate, and he felt self-loathing rise up like bile to swamp him.

He knew he ought to apologise, but there weren't any words he could think of that would make things better, so he stayed silent while she watched him.

After a moment she struggled upright and walked over to the rain-lashed window, staring out into the chilly night while she nursed her brandy.

'How?' she asked after a long while, and he didn't pretend not to understand.

'Cancer,' he said succinctly. 'He refused a gastrectomy last October. That's when I took over the practice. But you know all that—'

She shook her head. 'No. No, he told me nothing. I knew he hadn't been well—he told me he had ulcers and that you had taken over just until he was better, but he didn't say anything about giving up, or…or…'

'Dying?' Sam said quietly, and watched as a shudder ran through her delicate frame.

When she spoke her voice was a harsh whisper, a mere thread of sound against the beating of the rain on the glass. 'When?'

Sam ran his hand wearily over his face. 'Two weeks ago tomorrow—in the early hours of Saturday morning.'

She shifted restlessly for a moment and then was still again, as if she wanted to run away and was holding herself there by a superhuman effort. 'Did—did he know?'

'Oh, yes. I think he knew almost from the beginning. At first he might have thought he had ulcers, but I think he must have realised quite quickly that it was more serious. He went into hospital in October for a gastroscopy, which confirmed it, but he knew it was too late. His actual death was caused by pneumonia, but it was only a matter of days.' Sam paused, then added gently, 'He was ready to go.'

Lydia nodded. 'Yes, I can imagine. He hated feeling ill.' She swallowed. 'Where was he?'

Sam closed his eyes, remembering. 'Here, where he wanted to be. He had a private nurse, but I got a locum in to cover when I knew it was getting close, and I stayed with him then till the end.'

'Thank you—'

'There's no need to thank me!' Sam snapped, much too harshly, and then more gently, 'I did it for him, to give him dignity, and peace. He was a good man, and I thought the world of him.'

Her shoulders stiffened as the pain knifed through her, and she turned back to him, her soft grey eyes like pools of mist in her grief.

'I think I'd like to go to bed now,' she said in a voice brittle with control, and headed towards the door at the top of the stairs which led through to the main house.

'You can't sleep in there,' he told her, 'the power's off and the place will be damp and freezing. Have my bed. I'll sleep here on the sofa.'

He thrust open the bedroom door and flicked on the light. The quilt was rumpled where he had sat on it to tie his shoes, and his dressing-gown was flung over the foot of the bed, but it looked soft and inviting. She nodded briefly.

'I'll bring your cases up—I put them in the surgery,' he murmured, and left her to it.

Lydia sat down on the edge of the bed and stared blindly at her feet. She couldn't believe that Gramps was gone, that she would never again hear his big, hearty laugh or feel the warmth of his arms around her. He had always been there for her, when everything else had failed her, when her father had gone off and left her and her mother alone, when the pain had become too much and her mother had taken her life—always, through it all, he had been there to catch her when she fell and kiss her better. And now...

She was dimly aware of Sam coming back into the room, of him helping her to her feet and easing off her mac, and then, when she still stood there, taking off her blouse and skirt as well, then pushing her gently down on to the bed and covering her with the quilt.

She was shaking, either from the cold or from shock, and he came back moments later with a hot water-bottle which he tucked into her arms. She thought he smoothed back the hair from her face, but she wasn't sure because the touch was

26

so light and she seemed disconnected from her body, as if it belonged to someone else.

Gradually her shudders died away and sleep claimed her exhausted mind.

Sam turned off the light, pulled the door to and gave the sofa a dirty look. Pulling pillows and blankets out of the cupboard on the landing, he undressed to his briefs and wrapped himself in the blankets, stretching out as well as he could on the inadequately short two-seater.

By the time he had eaten the stew had been dried up and the potato hard as iron. Hunger chewed at his insides and guilt tortured his conscience.

It had taken him all of ten seconds to realise that he had made a dreadful mistake, that, for all her faults, and he was sure she must be riddled with them, she was not a gold-digger and her distress at her grandfather's death had been not only genuine but frighteningly deep.

He had been quite worried about her when he had come up with her luggage, but she seemed to be sleeping now. He would have to apologise in the morning for the way he had broken the news to her, but he really believed she should have had his letters, the first telling her to come home to her grandfather, the second informing her of the date of the funeral.

He shifted on to his back, propped his legs on the table and crossed his arms over his chest. She still should have been here! She should have realised that he was ill and needed her. Damn it, day after day the old man had asked for her! If Sam had only realised that she hadn't known he would have sent for her sooner.

The moon broke through a hole in the clouds and tracked steadily across the sky, and Sam lay and watched it, and wondered why old Dr Moore hadn't told Lydia that he was dying.

He woke suddenly when the room was still in darkness, and lay for a moment wondering what had disturbed him.

Then he heard it again, a thin, high moan, an animal keening that cut through him to the bone.

Untangling the blankets, he stumbled off the sofa and into the bedroom, but it was empty. The sound came again, and he followed it downstairs and into the surgery.

He found her, curled into a ball on the old leather armchair at the desk, with her arms wrapped tightly round a cushion, rocking gently back and forth while the terrible sound of grief was torn from her throat.

Her eyes were dry and sightless, and she ignored him as he lifted her from the chair and sat down with her cradled against the broad expanse of his chest. She was wearing his dressing-gown but still she was shivering, and he hadn't taken the time to pull on any clothes, so he stretched out and turned on the electric heater. It could be a long night.

Then, holding her close, he rocked her, brushing the hair from her eyes and pressing his lips to her crown as if he could take away the pain.

He could feel the tension building in her, and then suddenly the dam burst and the tears came, accompanied by huge, racking sobs that gradually died away to leave her spent and weak against his shoulder. She slept then, relaxed into the curve of his arms, and he stayed where he was, holding her quietly, until the dawn lightened the sky.

Then she stirred and sat up, embarrassed and bewildered, and he smiled slightly and let her go.

'I—I'm sorry, I didn't mean to disturb you. I couldn't sleep. I just felt...' Her hands fluttered helplessly for a moment before she clamped them together. 'I wanted to be near him.'

'I know. Don't apologise, I often feel the same. Would you like a cup of tea?'

She nodded. 'Please. I think I'll just wash my face—perhaps I'll feel better then.'

He led the way upstairs, and while she cleaned up he put the kettle on and pulled on his jeans and a jumper, suddenly conscious of his scanty attire.

When she emerged from the bathroom, her face pink and scrubbed, her hair brushed and tied back in a pony-tail, and looking about seventeen, he was shocked to feel himself respond to her.

Technically speaking, she was a scrawny little thing for all her height, weighing next to nothing, her face too small for those ridiculously large eyes, her mouth full and soft and vulnerable, and yet he wanted her. His dressing-gown was wrapped tightly round her slim frame, the belt accentuating her tiny waist. He was sure he could span it with his fingers, and his palms tingled with the need to cup the soft jut of her breasts in his hands. She should have looked ridiculous, but there was something about her, her quiet dignity, the graceful way she moved those absurdly long legs as she walked towards him, that lifted her above criticism and made her beautiful. Sam felt the unbidden surge of desire, mingled dangerously with the urge to protect and nurture, and when their eyes met it was as if she saw right through him, and he felt ashamed.

'Tea,' he said economically, and thrust a mug into her hand, taking his and standing by the window.

She sat down among the tangled blankets and sighed.

'I'm sorry you had to sleep on this; it can't have been comfortable,' she offered, and he shrugged.

'I've known worse. Don't think about it. You needed the bed more. I'll put the heating on in the house today and get it aired for you. You can sleep in your own bed from tonight.' He turned to face her, and found himself trapped again in the clear grey pools of her eyes.

'I'm sorry about your grandfather,' he apologised, dragging his eyes away from hers with difficulty. 'I didn't realise you hadn't got the letters. I suppose the post is a little primitive?'

Her mouth lifted in the beginnings of a smile. 'Something like that. And the clinic is mobile, so that makes us even harder to find. We only got the Christmas cards last week!'

Sam's shoulders sagged. 'I'm sorry, I—I would never have told you like that.'

She lifted her hand. 'Please, don't worry. It really doesn't matter. The end result would have been the same.' She fiddled with the belt of his dressing-gown for a moment, then looked up. 'Is his car still in the garage? I'd like to go— Is he buried—? Oh, hell!'

She fumbled in the pockets, and Sam thrust a handful of tissues into her hands and waited while she pulled herself together.

'He was buried in the churchyard. If you can hang on until after surgery I'll take you later, but first I have to go down to the village shop and get some food in before I can offer you breakfast.'

She nodded, and drained her tea. 'Do you mind if I have a shower?' she asked.

He glanced at his watch. 'No, do it now. The water's hot. I'll go and sort out the heating in the house.'

He disappeared through the door on the landing, and Lydia stayed where she was for a moment, nursing the still-warm cup and trying to sort out her feelings.

He had been so foul to her last night —understandably, really, if he had thought that she had come back just to claim her inheritance. And yet today he was patient, kind, understanding... She could see now why Gramps had spoken of him in such warm words, almost as if he were the son her father had failed to be.

Which brought her to the next problem.

Sam came back into the room, and she voiced her thoughts almost unconsciously.

'How long do you think it will take you to find another practice?'

CHAPTER TWO

As an opening gambit, it was not an unqualified success.

Sam froze in his tracks, turned slowly to Lydia and glared at her with hostile disbelief.

'Let me get one thing perfectly straight,' he said coldly. 'This is my practice. Understand? *Mine.* Officially, legally, all signed and sealed and recognised by the relevant authorities. It is not up for grabs, I am not going anywhere, and it is not open to discussion. If you want a job I suggest you pick up a professional journal and find out what's available—because this one isn't.'

He ran down the stairs, and she yelled after him, 'How dare you speak to me like that in my own house?'

He stopped halfway and ran back up, pointing at the connecting door. 'That's your house, Miss Moore. The heating's on, so's the electricity. I'm going to the village shop. I suggest you get your things moved off *my* property by the time I get back.'

He turned on his heel and ran back down the stairs, and a few seconds later Lydia heard the surgery door bang and then the revving of a car engine.

He shot off the drive with a spray of gravel, and the sound seemed to release her from her trance. She leapt to her feet and ran into the bedroom, wrenching off his dressing-gown as if she could distance herself further from him by doing so. Then she snatched up her things, dashing away the tears that would keep gathering on her lashes and clogging up her view.

Damn him! How dared he speak to her like that? How *dared* he throw her out? First thing on Monday morning she was going to see her solicitor to find out about the will, because one thing was certain—living next to him was going to be insufferable!

She dragged her cases along the floor to the landing, opened the door and half dragged, half carried them up the three steps to the main part of the house. She got them as far as the door of her bedroom, and then collapsed on the landing floor in tears.

Why was she always rejected? First her father, then her mother, then Graham; even Jim Holden had found someone to replace her. And now the one person who had always had time for her was gone, and in his place was a cruel, unfeeling career doctor, who was probably hideously efficient and hated by all her grandfather's patients. Well, damn him!

She forgot his kindness of this morning, his caring and compassion, the way he had given up his bed for her. Gone was all memory of his arms cradling her against his chest, soothing her until her grief had run its course and she was quiet. Instead she remembered only his harsh words, and the fact that he had thrown her out.

'Your practice, indeed! We'll see about that!' she yelled at the door, and, scrubbing away the last of the tears, she pulled on her clothes, ran downstairs to the hall and picked up the phone, dialling with shaking fingers.

'Hello? Sir James? Hello, it's Lydia Moore. I'm sorry to disturb you at home,' she began, all ready to launch into the fray.

'Lydia, my dear! How are you? I was so sorry to hear about your grandfather—a tragic loss to the medical profession, not to mention you...tragic loss.'

Lydia swallowed. 'Yes, it was. I wish someone had let me know—'

'We did try, my dear, but there was no time. The end was quite quick, I gather. And of course Dr Davenport was wonderful to him. Got a locum in at his own expense so that he could be with your grandfather till the last. Like a son—better than a son, if you'll forgive my saying so.'

36

Lydia could. She had grown used to the idea that her father had been a cruel and unfeeling man, but she really didn't want to listen to Sir James praising Sam, either!

He continued, 'Harry was extremely fond of him, y'know. They became very close over the months, and nothing was too much trouble. I understand he's left him the practice premises—very appropriate, don't you think? He certainly deserves them. What are you going to do about the rest of the house?'

Lydia frowned. In the face of so much praise from the chairman of the local branch of the FHSA, she could hardly criticise Sam without sounding whining and ungrateful, so she stalled. 'I haven't made a decision yet, Sir James. It all depends on where I end up working—'

'Nice little practice up near Diss needs a new partner—might consider a young woman, given the right encouragement. Want me to have a word?'

Here was her chance. 'Well, actually, Sir James, I was rather hoping to have taken over from my grandfather—'

'Yes, I know. Pity about that. Given another couple of years' experience, we might even have considered you, but it's a big practice, and very widespread. We'd even suggested that Harry should take a partner, but young Davenport seems to be managing admirably on his own. He's set up links with Hastings three miles away to cover each other's on call, so they've got their free time sorted out. Maybe if the population increases we could justify another post, but I don't think there's any likelihood of his leaving in the foreseeable future. However, Harry's patients all seem to be delighted with his successor, and I must say, from this end, he seems much more efficient than Harry ever was!'

Lydia sighed. More praise! Was there no end to the virtue of this paragon?

'I think Gramps found the paperwork of the new contract all a bit daunting—'

Sir James laughed. 'Don't we all, my dear? Still, if it helps to make a more efficient health service—let me know what you decide about that other job, won't you? It's a big group—they could afford to take someone without too much experience. In the meantime, we could always use another locum in the area.'

'Yes, I'll consider it. Thank you, Sir James.'

She hung up, her last hopes dashed.

Sam Davenport was obviously a well-liked and respected member of the profession already, and it wouldn't help her case at all to go making waves.

She wandered slowly through the house, touching familiar things, hearing the past echo in her mind, until she found herself in the conservatory again.

Tucking her feet up under her bottom, she curled up in the old wicker rocking-chair and stared sadly down the neglected garden.

She had come home before she had really got over the shock of Graham's defection, to take up the reins of her future with Gramps because she had had an uneasy suspicion about him—only to have her world snatched out from under her feet at a stroke.

Her unease had been too little, too late, and now he was gone; her dreams lay in the dust, trampled underfoot by a man whom everyone else seemed to hold in almost reverent awe—and who clearly despised her as a gold-digger.

If he only knew! She didn't want the terrible responsibility for the crumbling old house—God knew how she would maintain it. She supposed it was worth quite a bit, but it was entirely academic because she would never sell it unless driven to it in absolute desperation.

As if to press home the point, the skies opened again and she noticed that the guttering was leaking near the corner—well away from the practice end, otherwise no doubt the highly efficient Dr Davenport would have dealt with it!

Suppressing a shiver, she turned back to the house and walked round it again, this time looking with the candid eyes of an estate agent instead of through the rose-tinted lenses of nostalgia. Everywhere there were signs of neglect. It was clean enough, but the paintwork was old and chipped, the wallpaper faded, and some of the upstairs ceilings showed signs of damp, unlike the surgery and flat, all of which had been recently decorated and recarpeted throughout. She cast another despairing glance around the sitting-room.

Well, looking at it wasn't going to improve things, she decided, straightening her spine, and she needed something to take her mind off Gramps.

She found his car keys on the pegboard by the back door, and let herself out.

Mercifully the old Rover started first time, and she drove into Ipswich and found a DIY store. There she bought paint, brushes, wallpaper paste, a job-lot of sale wallpaper, a hot-air stripper and a wallpaper steam stripper.

Three hours later she was standing at the kitchen sink cleaning up the steam stripper and wondering what she'd started. The sitting-room was now reduced to chaos, and as for Lydia, she was covered in peeling paint and strips of soggy wallpaper, her jeans were caked with paste, lumps of gooey paper were stuck to her knees and she looked a fright.

She was not, therefore, terribly pleased to see Sam darken the kitchen doorway.

'What do you want?' she snapped, shoving an escaping tendril of hair out of the way with the back of her paste-covered hands, and jutting her little chin out in an unconsciously endearing gesture.

'I just wanted to apologise—'

'Good. Fine. Accepted. Now please go, I'm busy.'

'I brought you some food. I don't suppose you have any.'

Her stomach growled in response, but

41

she would rather have starved than admit it.

'I'm going out later, thank you,' she said stiffly.

'Really?' He dumped the heavy box down on the worktop and dusted off his hands. 'Well, now you won't need to.'

'Since you've already bought the things, I suppose you may as well leave them. You must tell me what I owe you,' she muttered ungraciously, and he gave a small, humourless smile.

'The receipt's in the top of the box. Don't lose it—I can appreciate that you would hate to be beholden to me!'

'Oh!' She glared crossly at him, and he turned on his heel and left, his mouth twitching.

She tried to remind herself that her grandfather had been a good judge of character and that Sam must, really, be a decent person, but she failed miserably.

'Everyone's entitled to one mistake,' she said aloud. 'Sam Davenport was obviously yours, Gramps.'

She screwed the tap off with unnecessary vigour, and screamed as the fitting came away in her hand and a fountain of water shot up and splattered all over the ceiling.

'Dear God, Lydia, what the hell are you up to now?'

Sam barged her out of the way, dived under the sink and rummaged among the pots and pans for the stopcock. Seconds later the fountain slowed to a steady well, and then stopped altogether.

He emerged, dripping, from under the sink. 'Pretending it was my neck?' he asked with a wry grin, and her sense of humour, never far away, bubbled up and over. Giggling weakly, she sagged back against the worktop and gave in to her mirth. Sam joined in with a low chuckle, propping his lean hip against the front of the fridge and thrusting his wet hair out of his eyes.

'You're drenched,' she said weakly when she could speak, and he looked down at himself, and then at her.

'So are you,' he said softly. Then their eyes met, and the laughter died away as he moved closer and brushed a drop of water from her cheek with the tip of his finger. He traced its path down her cheek, and then with his finger he tipped up her chin and looked down into her eyes.

'Thank you for rescuing me,' Lydia murmured breathlessly, and watched in

43

fascination as his head lowered towards hers.

'You're welcome,' he breathed against her mouth, and then his lips touched hers, shifting slightly against them before settling gently but firmly in place. His hands came up to cup the back of her head, and with a sigh she relaxed against him, giving in to the waves of warmth that lapped around her.

But the sigh was her undoing, because he deepened the kiss, and the warmth turned to a raging heat that swept up from nowhere and threatened to engulf them.

His lips left hers and tracked in hot open-mouthed kisses down her throat, lapping the water from her skin and sending shivers down her spine. She gave a wordless little cry, and he brought his mouth back to hers, cradling her willing body against his and drinking deeply from her lips.

Then he lifted his head slowly, laying feather-light kisses on her eyelids, and, placing his hands on her shoulders, he eased her gently away from him.

'I'm really very sorry,' he said gruffly.

Lydia shook her head. She couldn't for

the life of her see why he needed to apologise for kissing her so tenderly and beautifully. 'Don't be sorry. It was—just one of those things. Anyway, I liked it—'

'Not the kiss. The awful things I said to you, the way I spoke to you. I hurt you, and I'm sorry. I never meant to. Can we start again?'

She was having difficulty thinking of anything but the feel of his lips on hers, the urgent need of his body pressed so close against her own, and his thumbs were tracing circles on her shoulders, turning her bones to water. She dragged her mind into focus. Maybe all was not yet lost.

'Does that mean you'll consider finding another practice?' she asked quietly.

His hands fell abruptly to his sides, and he stepped back sharply, his face twisted with disdain. 'I might have known,' he said bitterly. 'Women always use sex as a pawn, one way or another.'

She was stunned, hurt beyond belief that he could think that of her, so she snapped, 'I could just as easily accuse you of doing that!'

'Why should I?'

'Why should you?' Her eyes widened. 'Because we both want the practice, and you're trying to persuade me to give in!'

He gave a tired, humourless little laugh. 'Aren't you forgetting something?' he asked wearily. 'I already *have* the practice. And possession, as they say, is nine-tenths of the law. In fact, the way things stand, you don't even have a tenth in your favour.'

Lydia watched open-mouthed as he turned on his heel and stalked out of the kitchen, then she snapped her jaws shut so hard that she nearly broke her teeth.

She mopped and blotted until her rage had subsided, then she sagged against the cupboards and closed her eyes.

'Oh, Gramps,' she whispered, 'I can see why you were taken in. He's very convincing, and so, so smooth! Just like a diamond—hard as rock, and when the light's right you can see straight through him.'

She called a plumber, cleaned out the fridge and put away the food, and then wrote out a cheque for Sam, dropping it through the surgery letter-box.

As she turned away he opened the door and emerged.

'Did you want me?' he asked, and she felt a hot tide rise up her throat and flood her face.

'Of course not,' she said abruptly, and he paused for a second, and then laughed softly.

'Funny, I was sure you did,' he teased, and the flush deepened.

'You flatter yourself,' she muttered crossly, and turned away, but not before she saw his face crease into a smile.

'Are you going to be in?' he asked a second later, and she shrugged.

'Maybe. Why?'

'I'm going out on a call. Maggie Ryder's in labour and may need me before I'm back, and I'm supposed to be covering for George Hastings as well. The answerphone's on, and it gives them the cellphone number to contact, but it can be useful having someone here.'

'To act as receptionist? Sorry, Dr Davenport, if you want a receptionist you'll have to pay one. I'm afraid I have rather too much to do.'

She turned on her heel and walked away, leaving him tight-lipped on the drive.

'Forget it,' he called after her. 'I thought perhaps I could appeal to your compassionate nature, but I was obviously wrong.'

She turned back to face him, hands on

47

hips. 'And what,' she asked icily, 'gives you the impression that I feel compassionate towards you?'

One eyebrow quirked mockingly at her. 'Who said anything about me? I meant the patients. Why should you feel anything towards me?'

'Apart from dislike? Search me!'

His lips twitched. 'Later, if you don't mind. I'm a bit busy at the moment.'

He ignored her outraged gasp and swung himself behind the wheel of his car, a new BMW.

'I might have known he'd have a flash set of wheels,' she grumbled to herself, and marched back to the house, head held high, back ramrod-straight.

He roared round behind her, and tooted the horn just as he pulled level with her, making her jump nearly out of her skin.

His laugh rippled back down the drive as he roared away, and it just served to fuel the temper that had been building all day.

'I'll fix you!' she muttered, and, going round to the back garden, she found the old wheelbarrow and filled it with bricks from the crumbling shed at the end.

Slowly, systematically, she constructed

a barrier that divided her half of the in-and-out drive from his, so that it was no longer possible for him to drive across the front of the house. Then she found some whitewash and slopped it on the makeshift wall so that he would see it, and stood back to examine her efforts. A bit crooked, but it would serve its purpose.

'Well, if it's not young Lydia!' she heard from behind her, and, turning, she recognised Mrs Pritchard from the village shop.

'Oh! Hello, Mrs P. Just building a wall,' she said lamely. Suddenly feeling rather foolish, she rubbed her hands down the sides of her jeans and attempted to explain that, since the surgery was no longer part of the house, it was sensible to separate it completely to avoid any problems over maintenance of the drive.

'Seem a bit daft to me, dear. Never mind, I expect you young things know best, but I hope that nice Dr Davenport doesn't mind.'

'Hmm,' she mumbled. She was actually hoping that he would mind very much indeed—in fact, she was counting on it!

She eventually excused herself on the grounds that the phone was ringing and, having gone in, despite her refusal to Sam, she felt obliged to answer it.

The caller was a young woman whom Lydia remembered from her childhood, who was going frantic because her baby wouldn't stop crying.

'Lydia, I don't know what to do! He just won't stop—it's been going on for six hours! I must be doing something awfully wrong—'

'How old is he?' she asked, and established through careful questioning that the baby was four weeks old, had no history of colic, was apparently quite well, not suffering from constipation or diarrhoea, and had a normal temperature.

'Where are you, Lucy?' she asked, and when she found out that the woman was only three or four hundred yards down the road she suggested that Lucy put the baby in the pram and bring him up to the surgery. 'Dr Davenport's out at the moment, and I can't leave the house because I'm waiting for the plumber, but if you like I can have a look at the baby just to make sure there's nothing drastically wrong, and the break will probably do you good—me too. It'll be nice to see you again. I'll put the kettle on,' she added, and it was only after she had hung up that she remembered she had no water.

Shrugging, she ran up to Sam's flat with her kettle and filled it from his tap, then took it back to her kitchen through the communicating door in the hall and put it on to heat while she changed her clothes and dragged a comb through her hair.

Lucy arrived a short time later, with baby Michael still screaming lustily in his pram. After tracking down her grandfather's medical bag Lydia examined Michael carefully, checking his ears and throat particularly for any sign of infection, and taking his temperature and listening to his chest.

'He seems fine. Lucy, I think it's one of two things. Either he's eaten something which has disagreed with him, in which case he'll probably get diarrhoea very shortly, or else he's just having a paddy! Let's see if we can distract him.'

Picking up the screaming child, she tucked him in the crook of her left arm and rocked him against her, crooning softly.

Almost immediately his eyes fell shut and he dropped off to sleep, much to Lucy's evident relief. However, he woke screaming again as soon as Lydia tried to put him down, so she laughingly picked him up again and carried him through to the kitchen.

'Tea?' she asked over her shoulder, and made a pot one-handed while Lucy slumped down at the table and nodded.

'Please. I feel exhausted! I had no idea babies were so tiring.'

Lydia smiled. 'You're at the worst stage. The euphoria has worn off, he's not sleeping through the night yet, and the lack of unbroken sleep is just getting to you. It's nothing to worry about. Provided you can get through it, you'll be fine. Thank your lucky stars you aren't out planting rice every day with him tied to your back!'

They chatted over tea, catching up on the years since they had last seen each other, and Michael slept through it all without a murmur.

'You see, I told you it was just a paddy!' Lydia joked. 'I should think you were all wound up and communicating your tension to him. Babies are usually very tough little things, you know. They're awfully good at getting their own way—look at this! He's been cuddled for nearly an hour, and he's had a terrific time! You ought to buy a baby-sling and carry him next to you. That way you can get on, and he can be near you all the time. Where did you have him?'

Lucy pulled a face. 'Hospital. Daniel insisted. I would have liked to have him at home, but perhaps it isn't really sensible for the first one. What do you think?'

Lydia thought of the little Indian babies she had delivered in appallingly primitive conditions in some of the villages they had visited, and stifled a laugh. 'If the facilities exist it would seem to make sense to use them,' she said cautiously. God forbid that she should be seen to be giving Lucy medical advice!

'What would you do?' Lucy persisted.

'Me?' Lydia laughed. 'It's unlikely to affect me as I'm not about to have any children.'

'But if you did?' Lucy persisted.

'I'd go for a home delivery—but hopefully I'd be married to a doctor!' A sudden image of Sam sprang to mind, and she dismissed it hastily. 'Anyway, I'm the wrong person to ask because I hate hospitals—that's why I'm a GP!'

Just then the plumber arrived, and so Lucy left, with the now calm Michael sleeping peacefully in his pram.

After the tap was repaired the plumber departed, amid dire threats about the use of brute force and the unlikelihood of the system surviving another winter. Lydia really didn't think she wanted to know.

The phone was quiet, there was no sign of Sam and so she decided to go for a walk through the fields down by the old gravel pits, to stretch her legs and get away from the house.

Her grief, still very fresh, was catching up with her and hour by hour was sinking further in. Always a bit of a loner, she suddenly felt the need to be miles away from everyone so that she could come to terms with all the sudden and drastic changes in her life. Regretting her petty gesture with the wall but lacking the energy to take it down, and unable to face another confrontation with Sam today, she dug out her old waxed cotton jacket and wellies from the boot-room and bundled herself up in them.

There was a lane that ran behind the house, and she followed it for half a mile before branching off across the fields towards the copse. Stark against the skyline there was an old wind-pump which had been used in times gone by to pump water from the bottom of the gravel pit, but it was long abandoned and the rusty old sails now creaked forbiddingly in the gusting winds.

Lydia snuggled further down in her coat and tried to ignore the shiver of apprehension that ran down her spine at the eerie noise. There were some children running around near the edge of the copse, and she could hear their shrieks as they played. She hoped they would have the good sense to be careful.

Then she noticed the pitch of their screams, and she started to run, feet slipping and sliding on the wet ground, and as she got nearer the children's cries became more audible.

'What's happened?' she called.

'David's fallen in the water!' the nearest child screamed, and the shiver of apprehension turned into a full-scale chill of horror.

By the time she'd reached them her lungs were bursting and she could hardly stand, but somehow her legs dragged her on to the edge of the old workings.

Down in the pit, some thirty feet below her down a ragged, broken bank, was a pool formed by rainwater collecting in the

55

bottom of the gravel pit, and floating face-down in the black water she could see the colourful figure of a small child.

She quickly dispatched the two oldest to run for help and call an ambulance, and scrambled headlong down the bank, examining the situation in escalating dismay.

There was only one way to get to him, and she did it before she had time to talk herself out of it. Ripping off her outer clothes, she plunged into the icy water and struck out for the child. The cold knocked all the breath from her lungs, and for a moment she thought she would go under, but then her chest started to work again and she dragged in some air and forced her frozen limbs to work.

Grabbing a handful of his anorak, she pulled the child back to the bank and hauled him up the edge, slipping and sliding as she went.

His skin was a bluish white, his lips almost purple, and there was no sign of breathing at all.

'Oh, God, no!' she muttered to herself, and just because she couldn't give up without trying, and because there was always an outside chance that his sudden immersion had triggered the diving reflex, she forced her frozen limbs into action.

Tipping the child on to his front, she gently depressed his chest to squeeze water from his airways. There was very little, backing up her guess, and when she laid her ear against his chest, she could detect a faint heartbeat every few seconds.

'Severe bradycardia, pulseless, no breathing apparent,' she recited, and, flipping him on to his back, she gently tipped his head back and, covering his nose and mouth with her lips, she breathed carefully into his tiny lungs. After two breaths she crossed her hands over the bottom of his breastbone and pumped steadily fifteen times, then gave two more breaths and pumped again.

After a few minutes she heard scrambling behind her, but she was too busy counting to pay attention.

'For heaven's sake, woman, you'll freeze to death!' a man's voice said, and Lydia became aware that she was still dressed only in her underwear, and the biting wind was chilling her body rapidly.

'Press here, like this,' she said, and while the man took over she dived into her clothes and then pushed him out of the way, continuing the massage.

'She's wasting her time. Anyone can see he's dead—look at him!' one of the other bystanders said in an awed voice, and Lydia shot him a black look.

'Not yet, he isn't. Not until I say so. Go and look out for the ambulance, please, so they don't waste time trying to find us.'

She turned her attention back to the child, counting fifteen pumps, then two breaths, fifteen pumps, two breaths, until suddenly a pair of large warm hands closed over hers and a reassuring voice murmured, 'Take over the top end. One to five.'

Lydia had never been so glad to see anyone in all her life.

CHAPTER THREE

They worked well as a team, Sam pumping the child's chest, Lydia breathing gently into his lungs during the pauses. It was much easier with two, and Lydia was able to use the intervals between breathing to strip off David's wet clothes and wrap him in her coat.

Someone produced a car rug, and they tucked it loosely round him to prevent any further chilling, although he was beyond the point where he could warm himself up. His only hope was that his body had gone into the primitive diving reflex as Lydia had supposed, and that his body's need for oxygen had been drastically reduced as a result. All they could do was keep his blood oxygenated and circulating until the ambulancemen arrived.

'We're not getting him back; he needs atropine,' Sam muttered. 'Can you take over while I give it to him?'

She nodded and went back to the fifteen-two rhythm while Sam drew up and administered the injection; then they paused to reassess the boy's condition.

Sam's eyes closed in relief as he picked up a heartbeat with his stethoscope, and as they watched the boy's chest lifted slightly with a spontaneous breath.

'He's alive!' someone called, and a great cheer went up.

Sam gave them a grim smile. 'Don't get too excited. We could still lose him, but at least he's fighting now.'

Slowly, as if he was calling himself back from a great distance, the child recovered consciousness and stared around him in bewilderment.

'Mum?' he said shakily, and Sam smoothed his hair back from his face and spoke quietly to him. He obviously knew the boy well, and Lydia wondered how often he had had to deal with him in the past. She had noticed the fresh sutures in his hand under a filthy, tattered dressing, and there were other scars and bruises on his skinny little body that worried her.

If he survived this crisis she resolved to discuss him with Sam, because she was sure there was more to his history than met the eye.

She watched silently as Sam undid his coat, then wrapped the boy up more firmly in the blanket and lifted him on to his lap, one arm cradling him securely against the warm, hard expanse of his chest as he rubbed the frozen little limbs firmly with his other hand.

Lydia felt a sudden painful rush of memory. She knew from recent and poignant experience how good it felt to nestle there in the shelter of his arms.

A shudder ran through her, and Sam narrowed his eyes and looked at her keenly.

'Are you OK?'

She nodded. 'Just cold. The water's freezing.'

A quick frown creased his brow. 'Did you go in?'

She nodded again. 'He was floating near the far side. There was no other way to get to him. It's very deep.' Once again she was struck by the horror of the cold water closing in and squeezing the air from her lungs, and she shuddered with reaction. 'I thought...for a moment...it was so hard to breathe,' she whispered, and shut her eyes tight.

She felt his hand grip hers, and his warmth and strength reached out to flow into her, filling her with courage. 'Just hang in there a little longer,' he murmured reassuringly, and she wrapped her arms around her chest and tried to keep warm until the ambulance came to take David away.

She heard Sam outlining the treatment given, including the point three milligrammes of atropine IV, and from his questioning of bystanders she gathered that he had been given resuscitation for at least twenty-five minutes—most of it by her, alone—before he had regained consciousness. It hadn't seemed that long, and yet in a way it seemed as if they had fought for him forever, she thought wearily.

David's mother had arrived, almost hysterical with worry. Sam calmed her down and then the ambulance was off, siren going, speeding the child to hospital and leaving an aimless gaggle of villagers, unsure what to do next.

They parted like the Red Sea, murmuring praise and thanks as Sam put his arm around her shoulders and led her, shivering violently, out of the gravel pit and over to his car. Her filthy coat he flung in the boot, and then he pushed her, protesting, into the front seat.

'But I'll wreck the upholstery—I'm all muddy!' she wailed, and he grinned.

'So am I. So what? Damn the upholstery. We just saved a child's life.'

His grin was infectious. 'We did, didn't we?' she replied, her mouth curling at the corners. 'How about that?'

Sam's laugh was warm and wonderful, almost as wonderful as the blast of warm air from the heater. Snuggling down into the seat, she closed her eyes and let her teeth chatter all the way back to the house.

It was only as Sam swung in and slammed on the brakes that she remembered the wall.

'What the blazes—where did that come from?' he asked, his voice abrupt with amazement. Lydia slid further down the seat and dared a sideways look at his stunned face.

'I'm afraid I did it.'

He turned to her in astonishment. 'But why? That's ridiculous! I need to be able to get in and out—'

'You could always reverse,' she offered helplessly, and hid a smile at his snort of contempt.

'I suppose you're going to build a wall all down the garden, too?'

She shot up in her seat at that. 'Did he leave you part of the garden?'

Sam shrugged. 'I really don't know. I haven't bothered to find out.'

'Then perhaps I should,' Lydia commented thoughtfully, and then added, with a sideways look, 'You may not, of course, be entitled to the drive either. That would make life interesting. You'd have to rig up a catapult to get the patients in and out!'

'I think you've got hypothermia,' Sam said drily, and, swinging his lean body out of the car, he came round to open Lydia's door and help her out.

As she stood the events of the past twenty-four hours caught up with her and she swayed against him, clutching blindly at his arms to steady herself.

'Dizzy?' he asked, his breath warm against her ear, and she nodded and continued to cling to him, headily conscious of his rough cheek brushing her temple. Her nose was buried in the soft hollow at the base of his throat, and as she breathed in her senses were teased with the heady mixture of soap and warm male skin.

His arms were firm beneath her fingertips, and she could feel the muscles ripple as he reached round her to pull her against him. It did nothing to restore her sense of balance.

'Lean on me, love,' he murmured, and she could have sworn that his voice was unexpectedly tender. Ridiculous tears sprang to her eyes, and she straightened away from him and moved towards the house before she made a total fool of herself.

'I'm OK now,' she said shakily, and she heard the car doors slam behind her, then

64

the gravel scrunch as Sam caught up with her in a few strides.

'Come up to the flat; let me make sure you're really all right,' he said, and, grasping her elbow, he led her firmly towards the side-door.

Once they were up there he sat her down on the sofa and then switched on the kettle. 'Cup of tea,' he said, and then came and sat beside her, opening his medical bag with one hand while he checked her pulse with the other.

'I'm fine,' she protested, but he just smiled and carried on, checking her blood-pressure and temperature as well. 'Bit low—just under thirty-six. Right, hot bath, cup of tea and a nice, lazy evening in front of the telly. Sound good?'

She laughed, a low, soft sound with a power she was quite unaware of. 'Sounds terrific.'

'Good.' He rose to his feet. 'You go and have a bath, and I'll make the tea. Go on.'

She stared at him stupidly. 'I haven't got any hot water, because the plumber's only just been and I turned the immersion heater off just to be on the safe side. Damn, I'll have to wait.'

He shook his head. 'No, you can't wait. You've got to get warm, Lydia. Use my bath.'

He walked into the bathroom and started running the water. She followed him in; the room seemed shrunken by his presence, and she had to use all her will-power not to flatten herself against the wall to avoid him.

'There. Make it warm to start with, and then add more hot gradually as you get used to it. Oh, and don't lock the door—just to be on the safe side.'

It all depended, Lydia supposed as he brushed past her, on one's definition of safety!

He handed her a huge, fluffy towel, thick and soft and sweet-smelling, and pulled the door shut behind him. Deliberately ignoring the sound of his movements on the other side of the door, she stripped off her muddy clothes and stepped carefully into the soothing water. Ecstasy!

She soaked for ten minutes, then topped up the water and lay back again, almost hypnotised by the sensation. Back to the womb, she thought lazily.

'OK?' he called, and she mumbled indistinctly. 'Want some tea?'

'Please! I'll come out—'

'No need; stay there a bit longer,' he said, and walked calmly in, put the tea down on the corner of the bath and walked out again, completely ignoring her panicky attempts to cover herself.

She told herself he was a doctor, that it didn't matter, he had seen millions of women in a worse state—well, not millions, she conceded, but enough—but somehow she couldn't forget the smell of his skin, the feel of his arms around her, the warmth of his lips against hers when he had kissed her in the kitchen that morning.

He might be a doctor, but he was also a man, a virile, potent, healthy young man who was probably blessed with twenty-twenty vision, knowing her luck. She gave her slender body a disparaging look and slid down further under the water, her trance-like state banished.

'Not a curve in sight,' she muttered, and then had to ask herself whether she minded Sam walking in because he might have seen her and wanted her, or because he might have seen her and *not* wanted her.

'Oh, shut up,' she said determinedly, and picked up the tea, draining it probably faster than was sensible and then scrambling out of the bath and into the voluminous confines of the towel quickly before he could come back in. She had no desire to expose herself again to the brief, dismissive flick of his eyes across her body.

Wrapping the ends across her breasts and tucking them in firmly under her arms, she came out of the bathroom and bumped into him on the tiny landing.

He reached out to steady her, and his warm hands on her shoulders sent little licks of fire dancing along her veins. 'OK? I was just coming to tell you I've got to go out. Maggie Ryder's about to produce and I want to be there. Will you be all right for an hour or so?'

She nodded, confused by his proximity. 'What about the phone?' she asked, stepping past him, and was annoyed because her voice sounded breathless.

'The answer-phone's switched on, but you can get it if you like. The cell-phone number's written on the receiver so you can't lose it. I shouldn't be long.'

She retrieved some clothes from her bedroom and, warmly dressed, she snuggled down in front of the fire to watch television in Sam's flat.

It was curiously cosy. She remembered it always had been when it was their housekeeper's flat, and she had always found a welcome there. Even now, with all the tensions and obstacles between her and Sam, she found it a comfortable place to be, but how much of that was due to memory and how much to Sam's influence she was unable to tell.

He had spread his quilt over the sofa, and she wrapped it round her and wriggled down into it. It smelt faintly of him, and she breathed deeply and smiled, a warm, soft, womanly smile of absolute contentment that she didn't bother to analyse. The phone was blissfully quiet, and, with the hypnotic intervention of the undemanding television lulling her gently in the background, Lydia fell asleep.

Sam let himself back in quietly and walked slowly up the stairs to his flat, his emotions thoroughly confused. He had just witnessed the miracle of miracles, the safe and straightforward delivery of a perfect baby to a warm and loving couple who were filled with joy and gratitude. By rights he should be feeling marvellous, filled with the same joy and also a sense of pride in

69

his professional role.

Instead he felt a curious bleakness, a pervasive loneliness that reached out and touched every part of him. He had left the Ryders' warmth and happiness behind, and was coming home to an empty flat, its only ambience artificially generated by electricity and owing nothing to companionship and love.

By its very nature, the work of a country GP made for isolation, a distance from his neighbours necessitated by the fact that they were all his patients and entrusted him with the most intimate details of their lives. There had been social overtures, certainly—all too often, he admitted bitterly, by women with marriageable daughters or whose own marriages were in chaos—but there were no friendships, only acquaintanceships.

He understood, and most of the reticence arose from within himself, but still he yearned for warmth and companionship, for someone who could break those barriers and reach out to him.

Someone like Harry, he thought, missing him with a sudden rush of grief. The old man had been a cushion between Sam and the reality of professional isolation, but, more than that, he had become a real friend.

Pushing open the flat door, he reached for the light-switch and then stopped dead in his tracks, his hand falling to his side.

Lydia! He had forgotten her, forgotten the smooth line of her cheek, the tender fullness of her lips with the slight lift at the corners even in repose. She was asleep, curled up on the sofa in his quilt, her cheeks flushed rosy pink in the gentle lamplight. She looked soft, tender and unbelievably welcoming, as if she were waiting for him, and for a moment Sam allowed himself the fantasy.

He imagined her waking slowly, still dazed with sleep, and reaching up to take him in her arms. She would smile, and he would kiss her lingeringly, chasing away the sleep and arousing instead the fiery passion of her womanhood...

He felt a desperate urge to wake her, to bury himself deep in that warm and slender body and take advantage of her unsuspecting innocence, and desire stabbed through him like hot knives.

With a small sound of disgust mingled inextricably with regret, he shrugged off his coat, dropped it over the arm of the chair

71

and went into the bathroom.

Even there, her image rose up to haunt him. She had looked so beautiful, her sleek, clean limbs smooth and tanned, her pert breasts pale by contrast in the brief seconds he had seen them before she had hastily folded her arms across them, her eyes wide with surprise. His body leapt to life, and, swearing softly, he wrenched off his clothes and forced himself to stand motionless under the icy needles of the shower until sanity returned and Lydia's image was banished to its proper place. Only then did he turn on the hot tap and allow the warm water to stream over his aching body and soothe away the trials of the day.

Lydia awoke to a wonderful smell of ginger, garlic and lemon, and the sizzling sound of hot oil.

Stretching lazily, she untangled her legs and stood up slowly, then ambled sleepily into the kitchen.

Sam was standing at the cooker in jeans, a thick cotton sweater and an apron with 'Please Kiss The Cook' emblazoned across it. She walked over to him, grinned at the apron and planted a light kiss on his cheek. He smelt delicious, and her heart somersaulted quietly in her chest.

'Hi, Sam. What's cooking?' She sniffed appreciatively and poked the contents of the wok.

'Chicken in oyster sauce, prawn fried rice and bean-sprouts. How have you been?'

His voice was gruff, and he regarded her searchingly. It seemed impossible to Lydia that he was the same man who had spoken so coldly to her that morning. This man was warm and relaxed, and she felt as if she had known him for years.

Accordingly, her smile was open and generous. 'I've been fine. How's the baby?'

Sam watched as she dipped her finger in the wok and curled her tongue around the tip, sucking it with relish. 'Delicious! Answer my question, Sam.'

'What question?' he said hoarsely, and she gave him a quick, puzzled took.

'The baby. How's the baby?'

'Oh. The baby. Um, she's fine. Normal delivery, good weight, Apgar score of ten—super job. Mother's well, just a few stitches here and there to tidy her up. Any phone calls?'

Lydia shook her head. 'Nothing. It's

been really peaceful. When did you get back?'

'About half an hour ago. You were out for the count.'

Her mouth tipped in a little smile. 'Sorry. It's been a fairly lousy twenty-four hours, one way and another.' Her face clouded, and she turned away slightly. 'Anything I can do?'

He shook his head. 'Just keep me company. Do you want a drink?'

'No—well, something soft. I don't drink much, as a rule.'

He pointed to the fridge. 'There's apple juice, caffeine-free Coke, alcohol-free beer—oh, I don't know. Have a look.'

He turned back to the wok, and Lydia crouched down and rummaged in the fridge. She lifted her head and looked at him, and her breath caught in her throat. His thighs were on her eye-level, and as he shifted from one foot to the other the denim moulded lovingly to his lean frame like an old, familiar glove. She dragged her eyes away.

'What about you? What do you want?' she asked, and stood as he turned towards her.

Her hip bumped against him, and he

reached automatically for her arms, his body brushing against hers, sending little electric currents racing from all the points of contact. His eyes flared, and she felt herself drawn into the bright green-gold fire that came suddenly to life.

'Want?' he asked gruffly, after an endless moment. 'Oh, Lydia, you don't know the half of it...'

Try me, she thought, and stifled a hysterical laugh. Her lips felt suddenly dry, and she moistened them with the tip of her tongue in an unconsciously provocative gesture that drew his gaze like a magnet.

When he raised his eyes to hers his desire blazed brighter than ever for her to see, and her heart leapt in her throat. She knew he was going to kiss her, just as she knew the sun would rise in the morning, and she knew she was as helpless to prevent it.

Her eyelids fluttered down and her lips parted on a sigh of surrender, but then abruptly he released her and turned back to the wok.

'Beer,' he muttered, and she whirled back to the fridge.

'Right, beer,' she said when she could speak. God, what a fool! He must have seen her waiting for his kiss—but she was *certain* that he'd intended to kiss her. Oh, damn!

She almost slammed the fridge and stood up carefully, as far away from him as she could manage. 'Where are the glasses?' she asked in a strained voice, and Sam sighed and wiped his hands on his apron.

'Lydia, I'm sorry. It's just—you're too sweet, too naïve. You deserve better than I can offer you.'

'I thought you offered me the contents of your fridge,' she joked, and then she felt his hands on her shoulders, turning her towards him.

He pulled her gently into his arms, and she could feel the steady thud of his heart beneath her ear. 'You know what I mean.'

She did. Rejection again, yet again because of her innocence, only this time not because she was holding it back, but because she was offering it. She realised with a start that she had known him just over twenty-four hours, and yet if he had asked her she would have held back nothing. Instead he had been the one to hold back, and she felt shame burn her cheeks.

'Aren't we both making rather a lot of this?' she said with mock-brightness, and tried to push him away, but his arms were like steel bands holding her against his chest, and he refused to allow her to retreat.

'Lydia, look at me,' he ordered gently, and slowly, with a superhuman effort, she raised her eyes to his. 'I want you. Don't think I don't. It's been a long time since I had a serious relationship, and I don't sleep around. But I have nothing to give you, and common decency won't allow me to take what you so delicately offered. Even if you weren't Harry's granddaughter, I would be reluctant. That fact just makes it even more impossible.'

'Don't be so bloody condescending, Sam,' she choked out.

He sighed tiredly. 'Condescending be damned. In the past few hours you've had to deal with bereavement, my evil temper, a drowning child and hypothermia. That must have affected your judgement. I'm here, and you need to reach out for comfort. It's natural, but it's the wrong sort of comfort. I'll give you my friendship, willingly, but nothing else. I don't want a sordid little affair—'

'For heaven's sake, Sam! I thought you were going to kiss me. Big deal! Who said anything about an affair?'

He dropped his hands and moved away, returning his attention to the stove. 'Don't fool yourself, Lydia,' he warned. 'With us, it's all or nothing. Sometimes it's just like that. Well, it can't be all, so it had better be nothing. Now, pour me that beer before I die of thirst, there's a good girl.'

She did so, fighting the trembling of her hands and the blush that refused to fade, and then she found some plates and a couple of forks and put them on the worktop.

Sam dished up and then led her to the sitting-room, firmly seating himself in the chair on the other side of the low coffee-table.

They ate in silence, avoiding each other's eyes, and when he had cleared his plate Sam rose and crossed over to the telephone.

Hearing the name David Leeming, Lydia eavesdropped shamelessly, and quizzed Sam when he sat down again.

'How is he?'

Sam smiled tiredly. 'Sounds as if he'll be all right—this time. I've never known a kid get in such scrapes. I must say, I wasn't surprised to see it was him.'

'No,' Lydia said slowly, 'I had a feeling you would have been keeping an eye on him. How did he cut his hand?'

'Fell through the roof of the neighbour's greenhouse. He was up an apple tree retrieving a frisbee, and the branch broke. It could have been much worse. Last month it was a split lip from fighting in the school playground, and before Christmas it was a fractured clavicle from falling off his skateboard. He just takes continual risks.'

Lydia frowned. 'Any idea why?'

Sam shrugged. 'Mother's a good woman —widow; her husband died while she was pregnant with David. He was on the oil rigs. She came back here to live when the baby was born. They live with her mother, apparently. He always seems well cared for, and the mother is very loving. There doesn't seem to be anything specific, but he just—I don't know, he's always very defensive, as if he's hiding something.'

'Such as what? Do you think—is it possible the mother abuses him?'

Sam shook his head. 'No. Oh, no. There's no doubt in my mind about that. This all started in September, when he first went to school. Before then he only had the usual medical history. There's no pattern of abuse apparent.'

'No boyfriend of the mother?'

'No, not as far as I know. There could be. I'll have a chat with her while he's in hospital, see if we can get to the bottom of it, but I think the problem's something to do with school.'

He eyed her steadily. 'At least, thanks to you, there's a problem to solve. If you hadn't got there, or if you had assumed he was dead and given up, he wouldn't be alive now. Your grandfather would have been proud of you, Lydia.'

Her eyes filled with tears. 'Thank you, Sam. That's the nicest thing anyone's ever said to me,' she whispered.

Suddenly he was beside her, his arms around her, and she leant against him and accepted the warmth and comfort of his embrace. The tears she had held back since the events of the afternoon spilled over her cheeks, and Sam muttered something softly and smoothed them away, his touch gentle.

Then his lips covered hers, and she gave herself up to his kiss with unconditional trust.

After an age he lifted his head and pressed his lips to her hair, while their heartbeats slowed and their ragged breathing returned to normal. Then he rose to his feet and pulled her up, shooing her gently towards the communicating door.

'All or nothing, remember?' he said softly, and she nodded.

'Goodnight, Sam. Thank you for looking after me.'

'You're welcome,' he replied, and she could feet his eyes on her as she let herself into the house and closed the door softly behind her.

All or nothing. That was the story of her life, she thought sadly. And it seemed it was to be nothing yet again.

CHAPTER FOUR

Sam appeared at the back door at ten o'clock the next morning, looking exhausted.

Lydia frowned at him. 'Bad night?' she asked, her voice unconsciously sympathetic.

Sam laughed ruefully and ran his hand

over the rough line of his jaw. 'Does it show?'

'Yes,' she said baldly, trying to ignore the increase in her heart-rate at his piratical good looks, and thrust a cup of coffee in his hand. 'Drink this. Have you had any breakfast?'

Sam shook his head. 'No, not yet. Haven't had time. I was called out at four o'clock for a heart attack—'

'Oh? Who? Anyone I know?'

Sam hesitated. 'Mr Gooch, up Sandy Lane.'

'Really?' Lydia ignored the hesitation. She knew why Sam was reluctant to discuss his patients with her, but he'd just have to get used to treating her as a fellow professional! 'He used to be the village schoolmaster, you know. Will he make it?'

'Should do. It only seemed very mild; might have been just an ischaemic attack, but I thought he ought to go in for tests just to be on the safe side. I'd just got him admitted and I had to go up to Valley Farm—Ron Blake had fallen off the cowshed roof and broken his leg.'

'Oh, no! How on earth did he do that?'

82

Sam gave a grim smile. 'Trying to repair a leak before milking. I expect he was hurrying. Quite a nasty compound fracture, and the cowshed isn't the cleanest of places to do that, but hopefully he won't get an infection, and he shouldn't be left with any permanent disability. His wife's coping OK—I left her doing the milking, because by then Mrs Humphreys had slipped on the wet path and bashed her knees.'

'Ida Humphreys? Good lord, she must be ninety if she's a day!'

'Ninety-two. Grand old stick. She'll be all right, just a bit bruised. Hopefully that's all for now—they say things happen in threes. Perhaps the rest of the village will have a lie-in.'

'Fat chance!' Lydia commented with a smile. 'That's country life for you—they're all up at the crack of dawn.'

'Swings and roundabouts,' Sam said. 'The evenings seem to be quieter than in the city. I also popped in to see Maggie Ryder—she seems to have had a good night, and the baby's gorgeous.'

'Gorgeous?' Lydia teased, and he grinned self-consciously.

'I like babies,' he protested.

'No need to get defensive! I like babies too—it's just that men are usually indifferent.'

'Hey! That's a bit of a sweeping generalisation—'

Lydia cut off his reply by pushing him into a chair and placing a steaming plateful of bacon and eggs in front of him. 'Eat,' she commanded, and, perching next to him, she raided a rasher of bacon.

'I'll go up and see Mrs H. later,' Lydia said, and Sam frowned.

'Why?'

'Why?' Lydia licked her fingers. 'Why not? I expect she'd like a visitor, and I can make sure she's OK and doesn't need anything—'

'Are you implying that I'm not professionally competent?' Sam asked, a thread of steel in his voice.

It was Lydia's turn to look surprised. 'Good lord, no! I've always done it—'

'Lady of the manor?' Sam said scornfully.

'Don't be absurd! Why should you think that? No, I simply meant that if any of Gramps's elderly patients were hurt or sick I would have gone to see them and done a bit of shopping—that sort of thing, just

84

good neighbours, not... Damn it, how dare you imply that I'm some self-seeking kind of goody-two-shoes?'

She made to stand up, and Sam restrained her with a hand on her arm. 'Sorry. Blame it on lack of sleep,' he said, and smiled apologetically. It was her undoing, of course, and she sank back to her chair, huffing a little, and pinched another bit of bacon.

'Your penance,' she said, holding it up, 'for doubting my motives.' She chewed thoughtfully for a moment, and then stood up and washed her hands, returning to the table with fresh coffee. 'So do you mind,' she continued, 'if I do go to see Mrs Humphreys?'

Sam raised an eyebrow. 'Does it matter what I think?'

Lydia shook her head, laughing softly.

'I thought not.' He grinned ruefully. 'Actually, I think it's a nice gesture. She's lonely, too, since Miss Harris died. I expect she'll appreciate a visitor. Talking of which—I wondered if you would like me to take you down to the church this morning? Somehow, yesterday, what with one thing and another—'

Lydia nodded. 'Please,' she said quietly.

'I'll just change. I was going to ask you, but you look so tired—'

'I'm fine. I'll go and have a shave, and meet you at the front in a minute. Thanks for breakfast.'

He stood up and moved towards the back door, but Lydia stopped him.

'Go through the house, it's quicker.'

'Don't you mind?'

She paused, searching his eyes, and then smiled. 'No, Sam, I don't mind. I know I can trust you not to abuse the privilege.'

He grinned. 'But can I trust you?'

She laughed. 'Probably not. I pinched some water from your kitchen yesterday.'

His face, became serious, except for the wicked twinkle in his eyes. 'Did you, indeed?' he said softly. 'I'll have to think of a suitable punishment for that.'

Tension hung in the air between then, until Lydia dragged her eyes away from his and made herself breathe again. 'Enforcing it could be a problem,' she said, her voice a little uneven.

'Oh, I don't think so,' he said, *sotto voce*, and when she looked up he had gone.

She took a moment to steady herself. After all, what had happened? Nothing. Just another sizzling, mind-blowing example of his potent masculinity tangling with her nerve-endings without any apparent effort! She made her way upstairs to the bedroom, which had been her retreat since she was born, and pulled out a burgundy corduroy skirt and matching blouse, with a soft grey cashmere sweater to ward off the chill. She twisted her hair up into a neat coil at the nape of her neck, and applied a touch of soft pink lipstick—more, she thought, to bolster her courage than for any effect she might create. She found her boots in the back of the cupboard, and her serviceable black wool coat, bought for its timeless elegance, and made her way down to the heavy front door.

Sam was waiting, hands in his pockets, staring at the makeshift wall across the drive.

Lydia walked slowly up to it, embarrassed and ashamed and stood hesitantly on the other side.

'Sam?'

He lifted his head, and raised an eyebrow in enquiry.

'I'm sorry about this.'

His smile warmed the cold recesses of her heart. 'I do understand. Will you help me take it down?'

She nodded. 'We'll do it when we get back, if you like.'

He held out a hand that engulfed hers with its warmth and strength, and helped her over the wall. There was something symbolic in that stride, she thought as she joined him. One small step for man...

They walked down to the church as it was such a lovely morning. Matins was in progress when they got there, and they walked round the churchyard to the sound of hymns filtering into the mellow air.

'He's buried beside his wife,' Sam said gently, and Lydia nodded.

'He would be.' Her heart was racing, and she stumbled slightly on the uneven grass.

Immediately Sam's hand was at her elbow, and it stayed there, a solid comfort, even after she recovered her balance.

There were mounds of flowers on the grave, from elaborate wreaths to simple bunches of daffodils, their stems wrapped in tin foil, humble offerings from the patients who had loved him. Lydia's eyes filled and tears spilled silently down her cheeks, and she stood at the foot of the grave and let them fall.

She felt Sam move away to give her

privacy, and she allowed herself a few more minutes of self-indulgence, then she straightened her shoulders, blew her nose and wiped her eyes, and turned towards him.

'Thank you,' she said, her voice surprisingly strong, and she saw admiration flicker in his eyes.

'Ready to go?'

She nodded. 'I'll come back later in the week and sort out the flowers and do something about a headstone. It will have to match Grannie's.'

Sam glanced back at the grave, his eyes bleak, and Lydia touched his hand.

'Are you OK?'

'Me? Why shouldn't I be?'

Lydia shrugged. 'You looked sad.'

He smiled slightly, and tucked her arm in the crook of his elbow. 'I am sad. I reckon he deserved my sorrow.' He gave a tiny laugh and squeezed her hand, changing the subject. 'Lovely day.'

'Yes. Yes, it is. We ought to get that wall down. It might rain later.'

They walked back up the hill in companionable silence, and as they neared the top he asked her if she remembered her grandmother.

'Oh, yes. She was wonderful to me. I was called after her, you know, and I think that helped, but she doted on me—spoiled me to death, in fact, though I never took advantage. I think I realised she was trying to make up to me for my father's being so—well, absent, really. She died when I was thirteen, five years after my mother, and Gramps had to take over then. We were all the other one had, and we leant on each other quite hard in the early days. We were inseparable. That was how I became interested in medicine. I used to go out on all his calls with him, and if any of the old ladies needed looking after he'd say, "My Lydia'll pop down and give you a hand with the chickens," or whatever it was. Grannie used to do it, too, before she died, and I often went with her then.'

'Have you always lived here?' he asked, sounding a little surprised.

'Oh, yes! I was born in the house. Gramps delivered me. Didn't he tell you?'

Sam shook his head. 'No, he used to talk about you all the time, but he never mentioned that. He didn't really go back before your grandmother died, come to think of it.' He hesitated for a moment, then continued, 'He told me you wanted the practice, but that he didn't feel you could cope with it yet on your own. I think he hoped you'd go into partnership with me—'

'But you wouldn't have me, would you?'

Sam stopped, and turned to her. 'No. No, I wouldn't. It's nothing personal, but I won't ever work with a woman doctor again. Once is enough.'

'And you accuse me of sweeping generalisations! What did this nameless female do to you, for heaven's sake?'

He gave a short, humourless laugh. 'It was an inner-city practice, quite different from this, and probably not the safest place in the world, but she knew that before she took the job on. Anyway, there was one particular block of flats that she refused to cover, day or night, when she was on call, so either Tom or I had to go, regardless of the time of day or if we had just spent the weekend on or what. She never asked the senior partner, Jock, to cover for her. I don't think he knew for ages. Then she said she ought to cover the ante-natal clinics and the well-woman clinic referrals and do all the smears et cetera—said it violated her patients to have a man interfering with them and I ought to respect that. Damn cheek!'

Lydia smiled to herself. 'Actually, in many ways I agree with her, you know. Many women feel the same.'

'But why? I'm just a doctor—'

'Don't be naïve! I wouldn't let you examine me unless there was absolutely no alternative.'

He looked astounded. 'Whyever not?'

This time she couldn't hide her smile. 'Because you're just too damn sexy, Sam. You could be smothered in white coats and stethoscopes, and you'd still be all man. That can be very off-putting. And do shut your mouth.'

There was an audible snap, and a flush ran up under his skin. Perhaps he doesn't realise what an effect he has on women? she thought. She suppressed a smile, and he glared at her.

'I've never heard anything so ridiculous. I'm sure your grandfather never had any problem—'

She laughed, a delighted, joyous bubble of sound in the mild morning air. 'Sam, you are such an idiot. He was in his seventies, with white hair and the most paternal bedside manner you could imagine. There's simply no comparison.'

He shifted uncomfortably. 'But men have been doctors for hundreds of years—'

'And women have had midwives for thousands of years. This masculine invasion of women's privacy is all very new, in evolutionary terms.'

He shook his head. 'You're crazy.'

'I'm a woman.'

'I'd noticed.'

They turned into the drive, and the wall stood there, reproachfully, in front of them.

Lydia grinned sheepishly. 'Truce?'

'Truce.' His voice was soft, tinged with wry humour. 'For now. See you back here in five minutes with your jeans on and we'll get a bit of equality going here.'

The wall came down much more easily than it had gone up. For all his talk of equality, Sam's muscles made the most significant difference, as he could barrow far more of the bricks away at one time. Even so, by the time they'd finished they had stripped down to shirt-sleeves, and Lydia felt sticky all over.

With the last load taken away and the gravel raked, they took garden chairs out of the conservatory and sat in the garden with ice-cold drinks from the fridge.

'Bit different from last week,' Sam said, stretching lazily. 'I must have a look at that gutter for you before it rains again.'

'If the weather holds I'll have a go at the front garden. I can finish the decorating on cold damp days. Then I must get in among this lot. What happened to Mr Riddle?'

'The gardener? He died in November—heart attack. Nothing's been touched since.'

She gave a soft, untidy sigh. 'They're all going—Mr Riddle, Miss Harris, Gramps—'

'The endless cycle of life, Lydia. There have been several babies born as well.'

He reeled off a list, including Lucy Armstrong's son Michael, and Lydia sat up with a start.

'I forgot to tell you—yesterday was such a muddle. She rang to speak to you in the afternoon. He wouldn't stop crying. I had a look at him and there was nothing wrong. I think he just likes to be cuddled, and he was picking up her tension. I think she was going down with a mild version of cabin fever. His ears and chest were all right, though, and he didn't have a temperature—'

'I don't believe this. You actually

examined one of my patients and then forgot to tell me?' He shot to his feet, anger in every line of his body. 'Damn you, woman, mind your own bloody business! This is my practice! Mine! How many times do I have to tell you?'

'But you were out! If there'd been anything wrong I would have told her to come and see you. I was only trying to set her mind at rest. Stop over-reacting—'

'Over-reacting? I'll give you over-reacting! I'm going down to see him now, and I warn you, if I find anything wrong with that child, I'll see you in court!'

The door banged shut behind him, and Lydia sat, stunned, staring after him.

'Well, of all the arrogant—'

Lydia stormed inside, oiled the locks on the communicating doors to Sam's half of the property, and locked them. 'See you in court indeed!' she muttered angrily, wiping her hands on an old rag and then hurling it into the corner of the kitchen. 'I'll fix him.'

She didn't see Sam again that day, and first thing on Monday morning she made an appointment with her grandfather's solicitor and had the contents of his will explained to her. It was painful but necessary, and she felt there should be no misunderstanding between her and her loathsome neighbour over the division of the property.

'So, although he has the practice premises and the flat, there is no mention of access? Does he have a right of way?'

'No. You can't have a right of way over your own property, so there's been none in existence until now as your grandfather owned it. As Dr Davenport's only just taken over from your grandfather, insufficient time has elapsed for a right of way over your drive to be established in the eyes of the law—'

'So?'

'So he has no legal right of access.'

Lydia tried not to smile. 'So I could charge him for the use of the drive for himself and his patients to gain access?'

'Technically, yes, although I'm sure your grandfather would frown on such pettiness.'

'I won't do it. I can just torment him a little—'

'You certainly take after Harry, don't you? He used to play pranks on everyone as a child, and he never really grew out of it.'

Lydia permitted herself a little smile. 'Just a tiny tease, Mr Fairchild. I'm sure Gramps would forgive me.'

The old man chuckled. 'I'm sure he would. He'd probably enjoy it hugely.'

They shared a cup of coffee and then Lydia returned to the house, dug out the old typewriter and concocted a letter to Sam, explaining the situation and charging him an exorbitant amount for the use of the drive.

She dropped it through the letter-box during evening surgery, and wasn't surprised to hear the communicating door rattle after the last patient had left. She heard Sam swear, then the surgery door banged and the knocker on the front door thudded down with unnecessary force.

Lydia opened it and leapt back out of his way as he strode into the hall, slamming the door behind him.

'Steady, you'll crack the paint—'

'I don't give a damn about the paint. What the hell is this?' He brandished the letter under her nose, and she sniffed and looked at it thoughtfully.

'What does it look like?'

'What? It looks like the biggest load of old—' He collected himself with difficulty, and glowered at her. 'What do you hope to achieve by it?'

'Well, you've got my practice, so I haven't got any income, and it seemed like a good idea to charge you rent for the drive. That way I won't have to work—'

'Damn you, Lydia, this is preposterous! I don't know what the hell your game is— Oh, no, you don't!' His hand snaked out and captured her chin, turning her face back to his so that he could see the laughter lurking in her eyes. His firm lips twitched, and he released her ruefully. 'Playing games with my blood-pressure?' he asked, his voice dangerously soft.

'I am angry with you, in fact,' she said, and moved away.

He followed her into the kitchen and stood awkwardly, fiddling with the letter while Lydia lounged comfortably against the worktop, arms folded across her chest.

'About yesterday—'

'Yes?' Lydia's voice was chilly. She *was* still very angry with him about that.

'I went and saw Michael.'

'And?' she prompted.

Sam shrugged. 'He's fine, of course. She went straight out and bought him a sling, and he was snuggled up on her chest when I arrived, happy as Larry. I should never had made those accusations. Mrs Armstrong told me you were at school together and that you explained to her that you shouldn't be looking at Michael and were only doing it for her peace of mind. I had no right to— Damn it, you might make this easier for me!' He glared at her, standing patiently waiting while he dug the hole and climbed in.

Lydia smiled like a tiger. 'It's easy. Repeat after me, "Sorry, Lydia, I was wrong." Go on.'

He gave a rueful chuckle. 'Sorry, Lydia, I was wrong. Now what about this letter?'

'What letter?' Lydia asked, taking it from him and tearing it into tiny pieces.

He let out his breath on a long sigh. 'Thank you.'

She looked up in surprise. 'What for? Surely you didn't think I meant it?'

He grinned. 'I wasn't sure, and I didn't really stop to think. But I am sorry about yesterday. I had no business doubting your professional judgement.'

'Did you?'

He shook his head. 'Not really. Your grandfather told me about your grades through medical college. No one picking up straight firsts is going to make a foul-up on a grotty-tempered little baby!'

'Thank you.' She changed the subject quickly while she was winning. 'Have you eaten?'

He shook his head. 'No time. Why, are you offering to feed me again?'

'Well, someone has to look after you. Did you have lunch?'

'Bread and cheese—'

'Sit down,' she commanded, and started to pull ingredients out of the fridge. 'Prawn curry?'

He nodded, and sat fiddling with the salt and pepper pots while she rinsed the rice and mixed the spices.

'I went and saw Mrs Humphreys,' she told him as she worked. 'She seems to be progressing well. The haematoma on her right knee is going down—it's a gorgeous colour. She's very proud of it.'

Sam grunted and poured a little pile of salt on the table, stirring it with his finger. Finally she sat down and laid her hand over his.

'Is everything all right?'

He looked up at her, surprised. 'Yes, fine—well, no, not fine really. I had a patient today—young girl, fifteen, with sudden unexplained weight loss. Looks like a classic case of anorexia nervosa, but I'm not happy. She tells me she's eating, and her mother bears that out, although she says she seems to have lost her appetite a bit. I thought then she might have bulimia, but that isn't consistent with the weight loss, and there's no evidence of bingeing.' He ran his hand through his hair and sighed. 'There's just something about it which makes me uneasy. It's too tidy, you know?'

Lydia nodded. 'Mmm. Sometimes things fit too conveniently. So what do you think it is?'

Sam frowned and shook his head. 'I don't know. Her periods are scanty and irregular, but she started late and may not have settled down yet. I told her to try to eat more and come back in four weeks, for further tests, but to come and see me immediately if she felt ill. She seems quite well at the moment, and she's quite chirpy. Maybe I'm just over-reacting.'

'Probably. Did you examine her?'

He nodded. 'Yes. Nothing. She seems perfectly healthy, just a little thin, but girls of that age often are. One thing bothered me, although maybe it shouldn't, and that is that she's adopted. I wondered—perhaps she wants to trace her natural mother or something. Maybe I'll ask her mother to come back and talk to me without her, just to get a fuller picture. Maybe she should see a psychologist.'

They continued to discuss the case over supper, and then the phone rang and Sam had to go out.

During the night the phone rang again twice more, and each time Lydia lay and listened as Sam left, and went to sleep again only when she heard the car return.

Later the next day she was weeding the front garden when he came out of the surgery and walked over to her.

'Another bad night,' she stated, and he nodded.

'I hope I didn't disturb you.'

Lydia smiled. 'I felt sorry for you. Anything drastic?'

He sighed and ran his hand through his hair. 'Nothing that couldn't have been dealt with earlier in the day if only the people had thought about it soon enough. It does make me cross when people are so inconsiderate.'

'Do you always go out?'

'Unless it's obviously unnecessary. I would never forgive myself if I made a snap judgement in the middle of the night and then someone died as a result of my idleness. I suppose that's why I'm a GP and not a plastic surgeon like my father.'

Lydia raised her eyebrows at the bitterness in his voice. 'But surely he has to work in the night sometimes, if there's an urgent case?'

'Face-lifts don't tend to be that urgent,' Sam replied, and this time there was no attempt to disguise the bitterness. 'If he ever got off his sleek and well-paid backside and did something for someone in a crisis I might be able to forgive him, but he sits in his Harley Street ivory tower raking in the shekels and criticises me for being a romantic!'

'I'm sorry,' Lydia offered, and Sam grinned.

'I didn't come out here to talk about my father. I actually wanted to ask you a favour.'

Lydia stood up and dusted off her hands. 'Ask away.'

'Well, I just wondered—we seem to be eating together all the time, and I

103

really haven't got time to cook properly. I thought it might make sense, as you aren't working at the moment, for me to pay for the food if you would cook for us both in the evening. That way I get fed and you don't have to find so much to live on.'

She eyed him thoughtfully. 'What's the matter, Sam? Feeling guilty?'

'Guilty?' He looked puzzled, and she widened her eyes in innocence.

'Mmm, guilty. You know, for stealing my job?'

His eyes sparkled with appreciation. 'Oh, that. No, not at all. You know how I feel about women doctors. Actually, I thought someone ought to keep you out of mischief—you know, put you to work in the kitchen where you rightly belong without all this emancipation lark that you don't believe in—'

He ducked the matted handful of weeds that sailed through the air and strolled, whistling, back to the surgery entrance. 'So I'll see you at eight, shall I?'

'I haven't said yes yet,' she complained good-naturedly, and he laughed.

'But you will. You don't want to eat alone any more than I do.'

He was right, of course, and she finished

off the flowerbed and made a meal to remember.

And so the pattern was set; for the rest of the week they went their separate ways during the day, and met up in the evening to eat and to go over the day's events. Lydia was making strides with the garden and the decorating, and Sam admired her progress and told her funny stories about the patients, occasionally asking her opinion.

She valued these times, and they reminded her almost unbearably of times spent with Gramps in just such a way. The only difference, of course, was that Sam was not Gramps, not by a long shot, and so the relaxation was not as complete, although much more stimulating and recharging than relaxation. The tension hummed and zinged below the surface, although both of them ignored it and kept it at bay, but every now and then their eyes met and the sheer force of their attraction was brought sharply into focus.

When she felt she could cope she went back to the churchyard and cleared up the dead flowers, replacing them with fresh ones and contacting a monumental mason for the headstone. While she was there one day towards the end of the second week, young David Leeming appeared at her side.

'Hello, David,' she said, a little surprised to see him. 'How are you?'

He grinned and scuffed his toe on the grass. 'OK, thanks. Mum said you saved my life.'

Lydia laughed. 'Maybe. I was just there at the time, David. I'm glad you're all right.'

David looked around, at the fresh grave, and then at her.

'Was he your dad?'

'No, my grandfather.'

'You got a dad?'

Lydia thought of her father, whom she had heard of last three years ago, at his death, and shook her head. How could she tell this child that she had never had a father, that, for all his father had died before his birth, he had been more of a father than hers had ever been?

'No, David, I haven't got a dad.'

'You're a bastard like me, then.'

Lydia was shocked. She felt she didn't know enough of the facts to contradict him—what if his parents hadn't, in fact, been married? Instead she concentrated on the other issue.

'Who said that to you, David? Was it someone at school?'

'They all call me that. Billy James started it. He hates me, 'cos I'm a bastard. His dad's in prison, but we aren't supposed to know that. Billy says he's gone away for work, but I know it's not true 'cos I heard my mum talking on the phone to her friend.'

'David, you can't hate someone just because their parents weren't married when they were born. That's what it means, you know, to be a bastard. Sometimes people use it like a swear-word, if they're being very unkind, but you shouldn't hate anyone for that, any more than you should hate Billy James just because his father's in prison. It isn't Billy's fault, any more than it's your fault your father isn't here with you now.' She straightened, brushing the damp leaves from her skirt, and smiled at him.

'Anyway, I'm glad you're better. You take care of yourself, now, and don't do anything so silly again, please!'

He grinned and ran away, waving over

his shoulder, and Lydia made her way back to the house.

After supper that night she told Sam what David had told her. 'Do you suppose that's what all the fuss is? Maybe someone at school—Billy, perhaps?—has got hold of the wrong idea and David's trying to prove himself all the time.'

'Could be,' Sam agreed. 'I'll give the mother a ring and have a chat, and leave a note for my locum to keep an eye out next week.'

'Your locum?' Lydia was amazed. 'Why are you having a locum?'

'Didn't I tell you? I'm going on holiday for a week, skiing. I leave on Sunday morning.'

'That's silly,' Lydia said, annoyance and hurt warring for supremacy. 'I could have done your locum cover for you. I know everybody, you've been discussing the current cases with me—surely I'd be the best choice?'

He shook his head. 'Sorry, Lydia, but you're the last person I'd let do it.'

'Why? Because I'm a woman?'

'No, because I don't trust you not to interfere with the running of my practice.'

Keeping a tight rein on her temper,

Lydia stood up, marched over to the kitchen door and yanked it open.

'Out!' she demanded, and Sam rose slowly to his feet.

'I would like to be able to trust you—'

'Rubbish! Get out!'

'As you wish.' He drained his coffee, smacked the mug down on the table and shouldered past her, leaving her simmering in the doorway.

'Bloody man!' she muttered. 'Who does he think he *is?*'

She hurled the door shut with a shuddering crash, and slammed around the kitchen until she cooled off. Then disappointment and a deep, unidentifiable sadness set in, and she made herself a drink and went up early to bed.

It was, she thought much later as she struggled for sleep, his lack of trust that hurt so much. After all they had shared, all the conversations they had had about his patients, she thought she at least had his trust—

Slamming her fist into the pillow, she turned over and lay on her back, staring at the ceiling, as the tears of betrayal slithered silently down her cheeks into her hair.

CHAPTER FIVE

George Hastings was on call over the weekend, and Lydia saw him popping over every now and again to collect notes from the surgery. Occasionally patients came up to the surgery to see him, and Sam was also in evidence until Sunday, so Lydia kept out of the way and finished off the decorating in the sitting-room with no great enthusiasm.

On Monday morning she saw Judith Pierce, the practice nurse, arrive in her car and park it on her drive, followed by Mrs Mercer, the receptionist, on her bike. Then a battered old Citroën 2CV lurched on to the drive and died, quietly, against the far wall, obstructing her garage doors. She should have stuck to her guns and charged him rent, she thought crossly. As she watched, a thin, lanky man unfolded himself from the rusting little car and headed for the surgery, anxiously checking his watch.

The locum, she thought with disgust,

and cursed Sam again. With her limited vocabulary she was running out of new ways to phrase her displeasure, and repetition was not her usual practice, so she abandoned him as a lost cause and attacked the garden.

At lunchtime the lanky locum strolled down to where she was working and smiled engagingly at her.

'Lovely day,' he offered, and she scraped the hair back from her face and glared at him.

'This garden is private,' she snapped, and he recoiled as if she'd struck him. Immediately contrite, she apologised and offered him a coffee.

'Are you sure?' he asked, a trifle warily, and she laughed.

'I'm sure. My foul temper is nothing to do with you. Come on in.' She led him into the kitchen and gave him a seat, and then ended up feeding him as well as giving him a drink. Why is it, she thought, that I always end up mothering these grown men? It turned out his name was Jack Torrence, and he had just finished his GP training and was looking for a permanent post.

'There's one going near Diss,' she told

him, and he shook his head.

'I wanted a town practice really. All this chasing about country lanes is bad for the blood-pressure. I don't know how Sam copes with this lot.' He thrust an address under her nose. 'Any idea how I find this place?'

Lydia frowned. 'That's the Leemings', isn't it? Is it David again?'

'Yes, he— Look, I'm not sure I should be discussing this with you.'

'Rubbish. I'm a doctor. It's just that this kid has a history—two weeks ago I fished him out of a gravel pit in the nick of time. He was almost drowned. He still had stitches in his hand from a previous incident. Look at his records.' She quickly filled Jack in on the conversation at the graveyard, and Jack's eyes widened.

'How the hell do I, a total stranger, go in there and deal with all of that? Why aren't you doing the locum cover?'

Lydia gave a humourless little laugh. 'My point exactly. Do you want me to come with you? I can say I came along to show you the way, and have a chat with his mother while you look at the boy.'

'Would you?' The relief in his eyes reminded Lydia of a drowning man clutching at straws, and she suppressed the urge to laugh.

'Just give me a minute to get cleaned up while you get the cell-phone.' She paused for a second. 'If you could move your car out of the way we'll take mine. It's much easier to drive yourself than direct someone else on these little lanes.' She smiled to take any implied criticism out of her voice, and was relieved when he accepted it at face value. She had no intention of going anywhere in his ancient death-trap!

In the event they would have had to take hers anyway, because his refused to start and he had to push it out of the way. Great, she thought, how is he supposed to go on visits?

They arrived at the Leemings' to find David up a tree trying to recover the cat.

'Last time it was a frisbee,' his mother said wearily. 'I've been meaning to ring you up, Dr Moore, to thank you for saving his life in the gravel pit.'

She grinned. 'My pleasure. What's wrong with the little rogue today?'

'Stomach-ache. He was sent home from school this morning. Doesn't seem to have affected his ability to climb trees, though,' she added drily.

113

'Mum? I'm stuck, Mum!' His voice was a wail of despair, and Jack responded to it by stripping off his jacket, rolling up his sleeves and squirming up into the tree with surprising ease.

'Hang on, son, I'll sort you out,' he said confidently, and with complete disregard for his clothes he inched along a branch and held out his hand. 'Give me the cat,' he coaxed, and David handed the protesting bundle of fluff back to Jack. Lydia saw him flinch as the terrified animal dug its claws into the back of his hand and clung on for dear life, but he said nothing, merely retreating cautiously and handing the cat down to Mrs Leeming. She set it on the ground, and it stalked off a few feet, sat down with its back to them and proceeded to wash itself very thoroughly.

David, meanwhile, was wriggling back along the branch towards Jack, and he grasped the boy around the waist, swung him up and over the branch and lowered him to the ground with a sigh of relief before letting himself down and dusting off his hands.

He ruffled the boy's hair, picked up his jacket and turned to Mrs Leeming. 'Perhaps we could have a chat?' he suggested. 'And I could do with cleaning up.'

'Of course,' she agreed, and sent David in to wash his hands.

She led the way into the kitchen, and Jack allowed Mrs Leeming to spread antiseptic into the scratches which the cat had inflicted.

'Wretched animal,' she muttered. 'It was perfectly all right up that tree, but he has to prove himself all the time, that boy. Still, at least we've got proof of one thing—his stomach-ache was all put on.'

Jack smiled. 'Dr Moore was telling me something about his history. She has a theory, I think.'

Lydia flapped her hand dismissively. 'Not a theory, exactly. Dr Davenport was meaning to discuss it with you before he went on holiday. David said something to me—I was sorting out the flowers on my grandfather's grave, and he asked me who it was, and if I had a father, and when I said no, he said, "You're a bastard like me, then." Apparently Billy James—'

'That boy!' his mother burst in explosively. 'He's just a little trouble-maker. Fancy calling David a b...'

She turned her head away, covering her

mouth with her hand, and struggled for control. 'I thought there was something going on at school—poor little tyke. He knows his father's dead—' Her voice shook, and she stood up and busied herself at the sink. 'I'll have a word with him.'

'In the meantime, what about this tummy-ache? I'd better have a look at him, just to be on the safe side,' Jack said, getting to his feet. 'That's the problem with things like this; because you feel everything has an emotional origin you can overlook real physical illnesses if you aren't careful.'

However, Jack found nothing wrong with David, and advised his mother to let him stay off school for the rest of the afternoon and take the time to discuss his father with him again. 'Perhaps some wedding photos?' he suggested.

Mrs Leeming nodded. 'Good idea. I always avoid looking at them, but perhaps it's time David and I sat down and had a good, long chat about John. Might do us both good.' She smiled at Jack. 'And thank you for rescuing him from the tree.'

'My pleasure,' he said with an answering smile, and Lydia had a sudden, crazy feeling that, given a chance, these two would hit it off rather well. Who knows, she thought, perhaps if he follows up the case they'll fall in love and solve everybody's problems at a stroke. And pigs might fly, her alter ego muttered back, and she stifled a laugh at her fanciful notions.

But it was not to be. Jack Torrence received a phone call during morning surgery on Tuesday to say that his father had been taken suddenly ill and was in intensive care in Oxford, and he came flying in to her, shaken and panic-stricken.

She calmed him down, removed Mrs Mercer from the reception desk and asked her to look after him and get him safely on his way, and finished off the morning surgery, a little late but still under control and within acceptable time limits.

The rest of the day passed in a blur, with visits, the routine weekly surgery at the nursing home in the village, and evening surgery. Lydia fell into bed exhausted at nine o'clock, went out on a call at eleven, again at four and again at seven, which got her back just in time for morning surgery again.

Mrs Mercer gave her a pitying look. 'Busy night?'

'Fairly. I'm not used to it any more, but it's lovely to be working again.' And it was. There was a spring in her stride and a lilt to her voice that had been missing since her return from India, and Judith Pierce and Mrs Mercer exchanged satisfied smiles and cosseted her. It was enough that she was Harry Moore's granddaughter, but they liked her as well, and that made all the difference.

'I always felt,' Mrs Mercer confided to Judith over coffee, 'that Lydia would take over from the old boy. You could have knocked me down with a feather when Sam got the job.'

'He's good, though,' Judith defended, and Mrs Mercer agreed.

'But he's not a Moore, dear. Never mind, perhaps they'll go into partnership.'

'I shouldn't hold your breath,' Judith told her. 'Sam thinks drains to women doctors.'

Mrs Mercer blinked. 'What a disgusting expression, Judith!' She became thoughtful. 'I wonder why? Do you suppose it's anything to do with why he's not married yet?'

Judith laughed. 'Perhaps he's just got more sense.' Her divorce had just been finalised, and she was enjoying her freedom. Standing up, she smoothed her dress, tugged her belt straight and headed for the door. 'I did wonder, though,' she threw over her shoulder, 'if Harry had that in mind when he left Sam the practice. Perhaps he thought, if he pushed them together... Pity. I wouldn't mind a quick tango with him myself, but I wouldn't like to get in the way of any master plan of Harry's!'

With a cheerful laugh she left the room, and Mrs Mercer stared at the door for several seconds. Lydia and Sam? she wondered. They had been spending a lot of time together, by all accounts. Maybe—

The phone rang, interrupting her train of thought, and after that she was kept too busy to speculate.

The week passed quickly, and except for a couple of incidents, uneventfully.

The first hiccup, on Thursday, was Ida Humphreys, who developed marked shortness of breath, dizziness and chest pain. Lydia found that her pulse was rapid, and her blood-pressure had fallen substantially. Since her fall in the garden she had been unable to get around so easily, and the immobility had not done her any favours. Lydia was almost certain that she had a pulmonary embolus, and arranged for her admission to hospital without any great fears for her recovery.

The second and more serious hiccup, on Friday morning, was Susie Parkins. Having heard so much about her from Sam, Lydia was interested to meet her in person. She was a pretty girl, with chestnut hair cut in a neat bob, and lovely brown eyes, but they were lacklustre and defeated, and her hair was lank and lifeless. She was also rather thin, although many adolescents were, and Lydia would have put her in the normal range were it not for her obvious air of being generally unwell.

'Hello, Mrs Parkins,' she began, smiling reassuringly at the mother, 'I'm Dr Moore, and I'm standing in for Dr Davenport while he's away. Do take a seat. Susie, come and sit here and tell me what's wrong.' She indicated the seat beside her desk, and as the girl sank despondently into it her mother spoke up.

'She's been feeling sick—I can't get her to eat anything much. I can't understand it—she says she's trying, but she used to have such a good appetite—'

'Perhaps we could let Susie tell me about

it?' Lydia said firmly. Mrs Parkins pressed her lips together into a forbidding line, but she fell silent, and Lydia managed to coax a response out of Susie. As she talked Lydia studied her, prompting now and then, and built up a picture of a confused, listless girl who was almost certainly clinically depressed. And no wonder! She was feeling increasingly nauseated, and had lost her appetite almost completely. Like Sam, Lydia thought of bulimia, and then dismissed it. She weighed Susie, and found she had lost another kilo—just over two pounds—and this in just little more than a week. The weight loss was inconsistent with bulimia, and Susie seemed to be willing to talk about her eating habits quite openly, which also was inconsistent. Lydia had dealt with one previous bulimia sufferer, and she had been bright and chirpy, and had eaten almost nothing in public, while maintaining a good weight despite her apparently inadequate diet—supplemented, of course, by her secret bingeing.

No, Susie was almost certainly not suffering from bulimia or anorexia nervosa, but she was certainly ill.

Lydia took the bull by the horns and suggested a total package of tests, including full blood count and liver-function tests. Perhaps she had diabetes or hepatitis, or maybe even glandular fever? There was still no physical abnormality revealed by examination, and her period was still overdue. Lydia also included a request for a pregnancy test, in view of that and the nausea, and then suggested to Susie that she should see a pyschologist.

By this time Mrs Parkins was positively bristling, but Lydia explained that, if they were able to eliminate as many potential diagnoses as possible, they would be nearer to finding a solution. She sent them away armed with bottles and containers, and carried on. Four hours later she received a call from Sir James.

'I've had a Mrs Parkins on the phone,' he said. 'She wants to know why the hell you've referred her daughter to a psychologist and why a pregnancy test is necessary on a fifteen-year-old virgin? I said I'd discuss it with you and ring her back.'

Lydia sighed, explained the history and apologised. 'I thought she was getting up a head of steam this morning. Can you calm her down? I really need those results, and I think she should see the psychologist.

She's in a bad way, Sir James, and she needs treating, whatever the cause of her illness, and however much her mother might hate the thought of Susie's needing a psychologist.'

Sir James sighed. 'All right, my dear, I'll go back to her and pour oil on the troubled waters if I can. You just sit tight and carry on. You're doing a fine job. Ignore her.'

'Thank you, Sir James,' Lydia said with a sigh of relief, and hung up.

She was annoyed, however, and all day long it stayed with her. How dared Mrs Parkins doubt her professional competence? At least Sir James had seen the light, but she had heard the doubt in his voice at the start of their conversation. Damn them all! She was a good doctor, conscientious and thorough, and she didn't need some neurotic old witch stirring the pot on her behalf!

Sir James rang again later, and said that Mrs Parkins was adamant and wanted a second opinion. 'I've suggested she brings Susie in on Monday morning to see Dr Davenport, and she's agreeable to that, so we'll leave it alone until he's seen her and come back to me. You know, it might have been better to have suggested she came to see him next week anyway, rather than rushing these tests and referrals. After all, not much can be done by Monday anyway. However, it's happened now, and I dare say no harm's done. Better to err on the side of caution.'

Lydia mumbled her agreement and hung up, frustrated and demoralised. Needing a boost to her ego she rang George Hastings and asked him if he could come over after evening surgery and have a chat. She dangled the offer of a meal in front of him and he accepted with all the alacrity of a reluctant bachelor.

She laid the table in the kitchen because the dining-room was still stacked up with ladders and paint-pots ready to be tackled next, and lit the fire in the newly decorated sitting-room.

When George arrived, a big, bluff man in his late thirties with ginger hair and twinkling green eyes, she was surprised to see him carrying a bunch of flowers and a bottle of wine.

'Ah, light of my life, it's been so long!' he said, and swept her up laughingly, dropping a kiss on her cheek. 'Here,' he added, releasing her and thrusting the flowers and wine towards her, 'these are for you.'

'Er—George, I hope you haven't got the wrong idea about this,' she began nervously, and his laugh and wink set her mind immediately at rest.

'Relax,' he said, 'I gave up hope as far as you're concerned when you slapped my face at your twenty-first.'

She flushed. 'You did come on a bit strong,' she protested laughingly.

'There was a lot at stake!' he replied, and gave her a friendly hug. 'Don't fret, my love, you're safe with me. Now what's the problem?'

Over dinner Lydia told him the story of Susie Parkins, and he listened in silence, interjecting the odd comment or question.

When she had finished he leant back in his chair, shoved his hands into his pockets and nodded thoughtfully. 'Tricky one, isn't it?'

'What would you have done?' she asked him.

'Everything you have—including the pregnancy test. Kids won't tell you anything in front of their mothers. I don't think for a moment she is, mind you, from what you've said, but you can't be too careful. No,' he pushed back his chair and stood up, 'I couldn't fault you if I tried, and I'm perfectly sure Sam won't, either. Now, how about some coffee before the phone rings and some hapless patient drags one of us off?'

They took the coffee through to the sitting-room, and were sitting on the floor in front of the fire laughing at an anecdote about one of George's patients when there was a tap at the door, and it swung open to reveal Sam, tanned and healthy except for a Tubigrip bandage on his left wrist.

'Cosy,' he commented drily, and Lydia flushed guiltily and leapt to her feet.

'Sam! You're back early. What happened —are you hurt?'

'Not noticeably. Where's the locum? The surgery door was open, so I thought he must be in here. Is he out on a call?'

She flushed again. 'Um—he had to go home—'

'Home?' Sam's face creased into a frown. 'When?'

'Tuesday. His father was taken ill, and I was here, so I took over—'

'*What?*'

'You heard me,' she muttered. 'I was on the spot, it was the sensible thing to

126

do—as it would have been to leave me in charge in the first place, had you been a reasonable human being.'

'Can't understand why you didn't, old chap—'

He threw George Hastings a killing look. 'What the hell are you doing here?' he snapped.

'Just soothing her ruffled nerves. The mother of one of her patients has been kicking up a dust about her treatment—'

'One of *my* patients!' Sam roared.

'One of *your* patients, then,' George agreed. 'It seems she couldn't accept the need for some of the tests, and didn't like the idea of a pyschologist being brought in. She rang Sir James—'

'Bloody hell, it goes from bad to worse! May I know the identity of this mythical patient?' he asked sarcastically.

Lydia sighed. She might have known he was going to make life difficult, and, anyway, he'd find out soon enough. 'Susie Parkins.'

'I knew it!' he exploded. 'Meddlesome, interfering woman! I *knew* I couldn't leave you within a hundred miles of my practice without you stirring up a hornet's nest with your incompetence—'

'Hey, steady on, old man,' George said with a frown, laying a restraining hand on Sam's shoulder. 'If it's of any interest, I would have done exactly the same, and if you hear her out I'm sure you'll agree—'

'Stop defending her, George, and get the hell out of here.'

Lydia stepped right up to him then, her temper frayed beyond endurance.

'*You* get the hell out!' she said furiously. 'This is my house, and if anybody's going it's you. Go on, out!'

Sam turned on his heel, marched out and slammed the communicating door behind him, and Lydia sank down on to a settee, her head in her hands.

'I don't believe I heard all that,' George said wonderingly. 'He's the most even-tempered, peaceful guy I've ever met. He must be in love with you or something.'

Lydia laughed shakily. 'Or something. He hates me, actually. He thinks I'm after the practice—'

George shook his head, cutting her off. 'Forgive me, Lydia, I am an expert on the reactions of single men. He was jealous.'

Lydia laughed again. 'Jealous? George, you're sweet, but I think you've finally lost your marbles. Why on earth should Sam be jealous?'

George pulled a wry face. 'I don't think that's meant to be a compliment, somehow.'

'Oh, George, don't be daft. I've known you forever! Why should things suddenly be any different?'

He smiled. 'No reason, but that won't help Sam. A man in love has a strange perspective on things, Lydia.'

'He's not in love with me, George!' she protested again.

He, raised an eyebrow enquiringly. 'Really? I shouldn't be too sure about that myself, if I were you.'

'Absurd! Save your breath.'

George eyed her thoughtfully. 'Perhaps it's reciprocated?' he said slowly.

'What? I think it's time you got an early night, George—your brain's definitely addled.'

'Whatever you say, my dear,' he replied with infuriating calm as he shrugged into his coat.

She kissed him on the cheek and waved from the doorway as he drove off. Just as she turned back a shadow detached itself from the lee of the wall and approached.

Her heart lurched, and then settled down to a steady thunder as she recognised Sam.

'What do you want?' she snapped.

'This,' he said, gripping her arms and hauling her up against his lean, hard body as his mouth came down to claim hers in a punishing kiss.

After a moment or so when shock held her rigid she started to struggle, and his kiss gentled, coaxing and soothing her into a sweet lassitude. Abandoning resistance, she melted against him, surrounded by his warmth, and when he lifted his head after an endless moment she stayed where she was, chest to chest, hip to hip, thigh to thigh. She could feel his heart beating in his throat, and she laid her lips against the rough skin under his jaw and sighed.

A shudder ran through him, and he put her away from him, detaching himself with a visible effort.

'I'll speak to you in the morning, and you can explain what's been going on,' he said tersely, and, turning on his heel, he walked quickly round to the side-entrance.

She heard the door shut behind him, and sagged against the porch. She had done nothing wrong, she told herself, even if her taking over had been against his wishes. She hadn't interfered in the running of his practice, nor had her treatment of Susie been wrong, in her opinion.

So why was he behaving like this, and why, more to the point, was she feeling guilty?

CHAPTER SIX

The phone rang during the night, but before Lydia could reach for it it stopped ringing and she heard Sam's voice in the distance as he answered it. Exhausted and unable to take any more aggravation, she turned over and went back to sleep. If Sam wants to deal with it, she thought, let him.

She was in the kitchen, nursing a cup of coffee and toying with the idea of breakfast, when the imperious rap came on the front door. Here we go, she thought. She tightened the belt of her dressing-gown, recognising the gesture as symbolic of the girding of her loins for battle, and yanked open the door.

'Good morning,' she said sweetly.

'Good morning,' he replied, a little taken aback. 'I wonder if I could talk to you?'

She opened the door wider. 'Why don't you come in?'

'Am I welcome?' he asked, a little tersely, and she felt her mouth tighten with irritation. She shut the door carefully and turned back to the kitchen.

'Not really, not with your current attitude, but I suppose we have to talk and now is as good a time as any. Can I get you anything? Coffee?'

'Oh, get off your bloody high horse and look at me, damn it!'

She whirled round and gave him the full benefit of her chilling glare. 'I beg your pardon?' she said icily.

'Lydia, I'm trying to apologise—'

Her laugh cut him off. 'You're joking? You call this an apology?'

'Give me a minute—'

'Why? So you can get in a few more insults first to make it more worthwhile? No way.' She turned her back on him and crashed around with the kettle, seething inside. Why did he do this to her? Every time they spoke they ended up at each other's throats. She supposed that in a way it was her own fault this time. Why had she interfered? She should have let someone else take over the practice—but who? She couldn't have let just anybody do it. He was quite right, he couldn't trust her not to meddle—not out of spite, but just because these were her people, her friends and neighbours, and she loved them all. How could she have stood back and watched their care suffer because the locum had had to leave?

She sighed and leaned against the worktop, her head propped against the wall cupboards. It had all worked perfectly well, too—at least until Mrs Parkins had stuck her oar in. Granted, there had been little choice, as the area's locum cover was running at full stretch, covering illness as well as holidays, but, even so, there had been no reason why she couldn't do it.

Until Mrs Parkins. Suddenly Lydia was assailed by doubts. Had she missed something obvious? She had to talk to Sam about it, for Susie's sake, because she had a horrible feeling that they really didn't have all that long to flounder around in the dark.

Taking a deep breath, she straightened

and turned back to Sam, and found herself trapped by his serious green-gold gaze.

He lifted his hands in a helpless gesture, and the corner of his mouth twisted in wry self-mockery. 'What can I say?'

The breath left her body in a rush. It was almost impossible to remain angry with him for long. 'How about, "I'm sorry I was so thoroughly unreasonable yet again"?' she suggested.

He sighed. 'I see our relationship stretching away ahead of us, a sea of misunderstandings and injustices, strewn with my apologies marching like stepping-stones from one crisis to the next.'

'That'll do for starters,' she said drily, and he gave a reluctant chuckle.

'I am truly very sorry—again. What I should have said last night was how grateful I am that you were here and willing to step in and take over at a moment's notice, and how relieved I am that you took such an interest in Susie Parkins, ordering all manner of tests to try and help her. Instead, I came in to find you curled up with George Hastings in a cosy little clinch—'

She spluttered with laughter. 'We were not in a cosy little clinch! We were sitting

134

in front of the fire, drinking coffee and sharing a joke—'

'I missed you.'

His words fell like stones, and in the silence that followed Lydia felt the ripples spreading out and warming her right down to the depths of her being. When he held out his arms she stepped into them and wrapped her arms firmly round his waist, hugging him tight, her face pressed against the rough wool of his sweater.

'Oh, Sam. I missed you, too. So many times I wanted to talk to you, to ask your advice. I mean, I know it's silly, because if you'd been here there would have been no need, but I just felt so isolated. That's why George came over, after Sir James rang, because I was riddled with doubts.'

'Tell me about it. Let's take some coffee into the surgery and go through all the notes.'

'I'll get dressed—'

He shook his head. 'Don't bother. Everyone's gone home, and I have to go out myself soon. I'd rather get on with it. The notes are already out—I've been going through them this morning.'

When they were ensconced in the surgery, Sam in Gramps's big old chair

135

and Lydia on the other chair pulled up beside him, she recounted the events of the previous week, starting with David Leeming and working her way through Ida Humphreys to Susie Parkins.

'So there you have it. The wrath of God is about to descend on me because I've asked for a pregnancy test on a girl who says she's a virgin, and who am I to contradict her? I just felt I had to cover everything. Maybe I was hoping that she'd lied and that she really was just pregnant, because I've got a nasty gut feeling about her, Sam.'

He sighed. 'Me too. Don't worry, I'll support your decisions on Monday, and we'll worry about her again when we've got the results of the tests. In the meantime you could do some sleuthing through the textbooks.' He flexed his wrists, and winced slightly. 'Damn thing. I could have done without falling over, but perhaps it's just as well I'm back early so you don't have to carry this alone.'

Lydia slid forwards in the chair and picked up his hand gently, supporting his wrist. 'It's very hot. What did you do?'

'Fell and rolled, and bent it under. It's

just a simple sprain, but it's enough to stop me skiing.'

'You should ice-pack it, to reduce the swelling. Come on, I've got some frozen peas in the top of the fridge—we can put some of them in a bag and cool you down for a few minutes.'

'It'll take more than a few frozen peas,' he said with a smile. 'God, I've missed you. Come here.'

He patted his knee, and she shifted across from the other chair and curled up on his lap, her head against his shoulder. She made a small, contented noise, and felt his chest rumble with laughter for a second before his fingers came up and tipped her chin towards him. As his lips came down on hers she sighed again and wound her arms around his neck.

As kisses went, it was only mildly passionate, but there was a warmth and acceptance there that made Lydia's heart overflow with joy.

Sam lifted his head and rubbed his chin against her hair, sighing with contentment. 'It's good to be home,' he murmured, and then his lips found hers again in another tender, lingering kiss.

She shifted against his lap and caught

her breath at the hard thrust of his arousal against the soft curve of her hip.

'Oh, Sam,' she breathed, and with a ragged groan he deepened the kiss, sending her reserve spinning away into the wide blue yonder.

'God, Lydia, I want you,' he muttered, and her heart hitched and then raced. She writhed against him, quite unable to stop herself, and his hand came up and found the open front of her dressing-gown, moving it aside. He captured her breast, the hard curl of his fingers gentle against the tender swell, the lazy movements of his thumb against her nipple a delicious torment. 'You're lovely,' he murmured, and, lifting his head, he stared down at his hand where it covered her breast. 'I can feel your heart beating,' he said, and his voice was shaking and unsteady as he lifted his hand away.

'Don't stop,' she pleaded, and he laughed untidily.

'I wouldn't, but you're leaning on my wrist—'

She sat upright immediately, her face flushed with guilt. 'Oh, Sam, you should have said something—I've hurt you!'

He stroked her cheek, and a warm,

tender smile lit his face. 'I'm fine. It's just as well. We were getting a bit carried away here.' He tugged her dressing-gown closed, and swallowed hard.

'Go and get dressed, there's a good girl. I can't bear knowing there's nothing under that except you. Anyway, I have to go now. I'll see you when I get back, and we can have some lunch and maybe go for a walk. OK?'

She nodded, and kissed him lightly on the cheek. 'I'm glad you're back, Sam.'

'Me too. You're good to come home to, Lydia. Very good.'

His words stayed with her for the rest of the morning while she bathed and dressed, enjoying the sheer self-indulgence of a day off after the gruelling week. She had forgotten just how demanding general practice was, and after she was dressed she spent a couple of hours catching up on the housework and shopping.

Sam came back at half-past one and snatched a quick lunch with her before going out again, their walk abandoned. She dithered for a while, and then went up to Sam's flat and found his suitcase, sorting out the dirty clothes and putting

139

them in the washing-machine with some of hers.

He returned just as she was hanging the last of them on the line, and she caught his frown as she turned.

'What's wrong? You didn't mind, did you? I didn't think you'd have time to go to the launderette, and I had to do my things...I'm sorry, I didn't think you'd object...' She floundered to a halt in the face of his obvious displeasure.

He shrugged. 'It's just—threatening, in a way. It's all so damn cosy. We eat together, talk together, you cook for me, now you're doing my washing—hell, it's almost like being married! All that's missing is the—well, the loving.'

Lydia looked away, her face hot, her eyes suddenly prickling with emotion. He was right, it was like being married, and she suddenly realised that she was playing house like a small child—only there was much more at stake. Sam was wrong, there was nothing missing. The loving was there. All she lacked was an opportunity to express it. The knowledge hit her like a thunderbolt.

'You suggested the cooking and eating together,' she reminded him in a level voice, and his sigh caught at her heart.

'Yes, I did, didn't I? Silly of me. I should have seen where it was leading.' He turned her round, and studied her with serious eyes. 'Don't fall for me, Lydia,' he warned gently. 'I'm a lousy bet. I'll break your heart if you'll let me. I've only let you get this close because I'm lonely and we share so many common interests, but I'd hate you to go imagining that there'll ever be anything more to our relationship than there already is. Perhaps I should start cooking for myself again—'

'Don't be silly, Sam,' she interrupted firmly, subduing the wild misery in her heart. 'Of course I don't expect anything more. You're a good friend, and I—I'm very fond of you, but you're quite safe. Let's leave things the way they are for now. We're both lonely, and it seems silly not to keep each other company. Anyway, I'll have to start looking for a job soon as you won't pay me the rent for the drive!'

He relaxed at that, and smiled at her. 'Are you sure?'

'Of course. I wouldn't say so otherwise.'

He studied her for a few moments, and then waved an arm at the house.

'Any chance of a cup of tea? I could murder one.'

'Put the kettle on while I hang up these last things,' she told him, grateful for a few more seconds to school her thoughts and get her expression back under control. For a while, this morning, she had really believed—Oh, damn!

She hunted in her jeans pocket for a tissue, and blew her nose, then pegged the last few items on the line and went back inside.

After that things settled down to their old pattern, with Sam joining her after evening surgery on Monday as usual and going over the day's caseload.

The only difference, other than the slight distance they were now keeping between them, was that on Monday Sam had seen Susie Parkins again. Lydia was worried about the outcome, and her preoccupation was reflected in her cooking. She burnt the casserole on the bottom of the pan, boiled the rice dry and undercooked the frozen beans.

Hurling the whole lot into the bin, she jumped in the car, went into Ipswich and picked up an Indian takeaway, arriving back just as Sam showed the last patient out and locked the surgery door.

'Hi—what's this in aid of?' he asked, indicating the takeaway cartons with a tilt of his head.

'Oh, I—er—burnt the supper.'

Sam sniffed. 'Yes, I can tell. What's that in there?'

'Chicken tikka and pilau rice, chapattis, mushroom bhajias and poppadams. OK?'

He grinned. 'Sounds great. Why don't I light the fire in the sitting-room and open a bottle of wine while you dish up, and we'll have it on our knees in there and be really decadent. George is on call tonight, so I can relax, and I must say I'm ready to.'

By the time they were propped against the sofa in front of the fire with loaded plates on their laps, Lydia's nerves were strung tighter than a bow-string.

'How's your wrist?' she asked, to fill the silence.

'OK. Getting better. I'll take the bandage off tomorrow, I think.'

The silence returned, broken only by the scrape of cutlery on china. Finally she admitted defeat and pushed her plate away.

'Sam, tell me about Susie,' she begged. He stopped, his fork in mid-air, and looked at her in astonishment. 'What about her?'

Lydia sighed. Surely he wasn't going to go all closed-mouthed on her all of a sudden? 'Did you see her?'

He nodded, chewed the forkful of food and took a swig of wine. 'She's just as you said. She looks much worse than when I last saw her a fortnight ago. I don't think we've got time to pussyfoot around and worry about the mother's sensibilities—that girl needs help, and fast, and if the woman had had any common sense the tests could have been under way by now.'

Lydia sagged back against the sofa. 'Did you manage to convince her I wasn't criminally insane?'

Sam smiled. 'I think so. I sent Susie out for a moment, and I told Mrs P. I would have done exactly the same as you in all respects, but instead of a pregnancy test, if she liked, I could have done an internal. I thought she was going to choke. She rapidly agreed with me that the pregnancy test was the least psychologically harmful option.' He grinned. 'Come on, eat up—you'll fade away.'

She pulled her plate towards her again. 'There's more in the kitchen, if you want some,' she told him, and tucked in again with relish, her nerves relaxed at last. Sam went out and came back with the remains of the meal heaped on his plate, and she finished off her portion and watched him wistfully.

'Want some?' he asked, and she shook her head.

'No, it's OK, you have it.'

He speared a fat piece of chicken and held it out to her. 'Open,' he commanded softly, and she opened her mouth and took the chicken with her teeth, tugging it delicately off the fork.

He followed it with a mushroom, a small scoop of rice and more chicken, and all the time he was feeding her a slight smile played at the sides of his mouth.

'What about you?' she mumbled through a mouthful of chicken and rice, and his smile broadened.

'I'm fine. I think you've been starving yourself.'

She nodded, chewing happily. 'Worry,' she mumbled again, and he laughed, a warm, commiserating sort of laugh.

'Don't worry any more. Mrs Parkins is all sorted out, and Sir James is quite happy.' He popped the last scrap of poppadam in her mouth and blotted her lips with a tissue. 'There, piglet. Better?'

'Mmm. Any more wine?'

He refilled her glass and handed it to her, and then leant back, pulling her down so that her head was across his lap and his fingers were threaded through her hair, kneading her scalp. She could feel the corded muscles of his thighs against the back of her neck as he shifted his weight, and the steady movements of his fingers and the warmth of his lap lulled her into a sensuous doze where the only reality was his touch, firm yet gentle on her skin, soothing all her cares away.

She felt the focus of his attention move from her scalp to her shoulders, and he took her glass and set it down somewhere before sliding out from beneath her and rolling her on to her front so that he could reach the tense muscles around her shoulder-blades. She was acutely conscious of the warm pressure of his leg against her hip as he knelt beside her, and the lassitude gave way to a delicious awareness of his touch. She lay beside him like a boneless cat, and if she could have done she would have purred with ecstasy.

After a while he rolled her over again,

and she dragged herself back to reality as he lay down beside her and wrapped her in his arms.

'Are you awake?' he murmured, and she nodded sleepily. 'I just wanted to explain why I got so ratty on Saturday when you did my washing.'

She snuggled closer. 'You don't have to explain,' she mumbled against his shirt, and he smoothed the hair from her face and dropped a gentle, undemanding kiss on her lips.

'Yes, I do,' he said quietly. 'Just listen please. I want you to understand. When I was at college I lived with a girl—her name was Jo, and she was a dedicated career doctor in the making. She was clever, witty, sympathetic, an excellent diagnostician and beautiful to boot. I admired her, I worshipped her, and I also loved her to distraction. She was destined for neurology, and I thought at one time that it was what I wanted, too. I hadn't even considered general practice, and when my father flung it at me as the only suitable option for such a grass-roots romantic as myself, I was stunned. I mean, I was going to be a brain surgeon or a heart transplant specialist or somesuch—not just

147

a boring, run-of-the-mill GP.' He chuckled, and the sound reverberated through his chest against her ear.

'Then I began to think about it seriously, and, as I tend to when I have anything major to decide, I hugged it to myself and sorted out my own mind before I mentioned it to Jo.' He sighed, and that sound too was carried through his chest, touching Lydia with its sad resignation. 'She was appalled. She wished me luck, packed her bags and moved in with my, best friend. By the time we finished our house year they were married and headed for a mutually satisfying career in neurology, and I was out in the cold.'

What could she say? Unbearably moved by his quiet, factual account of the destruction of his happiness, she could only hold him tighter, as if by doing so she could absorb the pain she could feel still trapped inside him.

'I finished my GP training, and took a job in Tower Hamlets, in a fairly bloody practice that gave me plenty of experience in a very short time. After a while I bought into the practice, and things went well for a bit until Annabel came along.'

'The woman doctor who snatched your

148

well-woman clinics?'

She felt him smile. 'The same. Then everything started to fall apart. I was having an affair with the practice nurse and, left alone, we might well have got married, but Annabel decided she wanted me for herself, and told Sarah a whole string of lies about me, including that I had been unfaithful to her; fool that she was, Sarah believed the lying bitch. I had it out with Annabel, and out of spite she then went to the senior partner and started making carefully phrased accusations of unprofessional conduct. She implied that one of the women patients had been a little concerned about the necessity for an internal. It was absolute garbage, and Sarah knew that because she was there chaperoning at the time! The woman had merely stated that she would rather have had the smear done by the nurse or Annabel herself, but I thought she had pelvic inflammatory disease and I frankly didn't trust Annabel to diagnose it. I didn't think she had enough experience, and Jock knew that, but he suggested it might be time to move on. He knew I wasn't really happy any more, and a woman doctor was useful to them with that ethnic mix; he didn't realise at that point that she was so awkward about being on call.'

'So you left?'

He nodded. 'What else could I do? I was so disillusioned by this time that I was ready to go, and every time I turned round I saw Sarah's accusing eyes or Annabel's scheming ones, and I'd had enough. I sold my partnership to an Indian doctor who could speak Urdu among other things, which made him invaluable in that part of London, and I started doing locum work while I decided what I wanted from life.'

'And you ended up here?'

'I ended up here, with Harry, and I've never been as happy, either personally or professionally, as I am now—except for one thing. I'm lonely. Harry knew I would be. I guess, like every other living being, I need a mate—it was lovely having you to come home to over the weekend, and, lying here with you like this now, I can't imagine anything making me happier. There's just one thing wrong—'

'I'm a woman doctor,' she finished for him, her voice tight with strain. It hurt unbearably that he was lumping her in with them. 'God, you go in for sweeping generalisations, don't you?'

'Do you blame me?' he asked, his voice tinged with bitterness. 'I've been hurt badly—twice—and both times by or because of a woman doctor. If I ever marry, and I don't know that I will, it will be someone unconnected to the medical profession. But it doesn't stop me wanting you,' he added, his voice husky with emotion. 'It doesn't stop my heart beating faster when I hear your voice, or my body crying out at night for your arms around me. God knows I want to trust you, but I just can't. I daren't. It isn't personal, not really. It's just that it takes a certain sort of woman to go into medicine, and that kind of single-minded detachment is capable of hurting as well as healing. Lydia, I don't want to be hurt again, I've had enough. It isn't worth the risk, and the only way to be sure is to keep away.'

'Oh, Sam, I don't know what to say—'

'Don't say anything—not now. I'm dangerously near to abandoning all my principles and making love to you, and that would be a horrendous mistake—for both of us.' He levered himself to his feet, and helped her up, smoothing her hair down with trembling hands.

'Thanks for the meal. It's been a lovely evening. Goodnight.'

He dropped a quick kiss on her cheek and left, his footsteps fading up the hall, followed by the sound of the communicating door shutting behind him.

Mechanically Lydia cleared up the plates, threw the cartons in the bin and put the fire-guard up before trailing up to bed.

Once there, she turned her face into the pillow and wept for a lonely man, too afraid to take the love she had to offer.

'Damn those women,' she cried, and closed her eyes, but still she could hear his voice, the bleak despair, the utter loneliness.

'Please love me, Sam,' she whispered, but only the night heard her plea.

The following day she rang round a few practices in Ipswich and volunteered herself for locum work. As luck would have it, one practice needed a replacement urgently to cover sick leave for the rest of the week, so she wrote Sam a note to say that she'd be too busy to cook and to help himself to anything in the freezer.

The week flew by, but Lydia found her heart wasn't in it. She couldn't understand how anybody could make a career of locum work. 'There's no continuity, no sense of responsibility or achievement, no follow-up,' she said to the junior partner, and he laughed.

'That's the attraction. No responsibility, just dish out the pills and move on. The GP gets to sort out any mistakes and pick up the referrals later. Obviously you have to be professionally competent, but it's a good way to get experience. I did it for two years, and I learnt so much, but it's a bit soul-destroying after a while.'

Lydia had to agree—after two days, never mind two years! She saw the week out and rushed back to Sam, only to find that he was away for the weekend visiting his family and George was on call.

The following week she took a couple of odd days of locum work, and in between she cooked for Sam and they chatted over the patients.

'David seems to be settling down,' he told her on Tuesday night. 'Mrs Leeming came in to get a repeat prescription, and told me that she'd spoken to him about his father, and that he seemed much happier since then. Hopefully you've sorted out that young man's problems.'

153

'I'm glad,' she said. She just wished she could sort out Sam's problems. She had missed him dreadfully, and was tired and dispirited after her locum stints. She just felt so disconnected from her roots—or was it from Sam, she meant? After all, she didn't know that many of the people in the village. Perhaps it was just her connection with Gramps and Sam that made it seem like home as far as work went.

'You look tired,' he said, and she gave him a weary smile.

'I am. Early night, I think,' she said without thinking, and was then disappointed when Sam got to his feet, dropped a kiss on her hair and left for his end of the house with a murmured goodnight. She hadn't wanted him to go so soon, but perhaps it was just as well, with the tension zinging between them as usual.

The following day she had off, and took ages in the morning pampering herself in the bath. Then she attacked the house and spruced it up, and spent a few hours in the garden weeding.

It was mid-March now, and the weeds were gaining strength hour by hour, or so it seemed.

By the time Sam came in for supper she

154

was tired again, but this time with a real sense of achievement. He, however, looked bleak.

'What's wrong?' she asked.

'Susie,' he replied, his voice weary, and her heart sank. 'She's got diarrhoea now, and, although her blood count and liver function are OK, it's beginning to look as though she's got some kind of malabsorption. There's a very high faecal fat content, which points to some sort of pancreatic or biliary disorder, but God knows what. I asked her if she had been eating a great deal of fat—I thought she was going to throw up. She's definitely not pregnant, by the way. I'm referring her to a surgeon—maybe he'll do an ERCP. Any ideas?'

Lydia shook her head. 'How about a sigmoidoscopy and barium enema?'

'I've suggested it in the referral, also serum amylase and further faecal analysis, but I don't suppose they'll show anything.'

'If she was jaundiced I'd suspect cancer of the pancreas—'

'At her age?'

'Maybe. Perhaps it's pancreatic insufficiency.'

'Could be.' He sounded doubtful.

Lydia sighed. 'Probably not, but maybe?'

Sam shrugged. 'God knows. She's gone downhill, I know that. It's definitely not psychological, I'd stake my life on it, but she's got her appointment with the psychologist for next week. We'll have to wait and see.'

They picked at their food, and eventually by mutual consent they abandoned all pretence of eating and went their separate ways, Sam out on a call, Lydia to bed to read up on gastro-intestinal disorders.

The following day she covered for two Ipswich GPs, both down with a nasty bug, and by the time she arrived home after evening surgery she was exhausted.

She was surprised to see that the surgery lights were still on, and George Hastings's car was on the drive. Putting the Rover away, she stuck her head in through the surgery door and smiled tentatively.

'Where's Sam? she asked curiously.

'Hello, Lydia,' George replied, locking the consulting-room door and coming out into the waiting-room. His face was grave.

'Is something wrong?' Lydia asked, her heart sinking. Perhaps his mother or father had been taken ill... 'George, speak to me, for heaven's sake!'

George led her into the office and sat her down, and then took her hand between his in a gesture of comfort.

'He's been in an accident. He went to assist at a fire at an agro-chemical works, and there was an explosion. He's in hospital. That's all I know.'

CHAPTER SEVEN

It was a nightmare drive to the hospital, and Lydia was plagued with fears for Sam every inch of the way. When she arrived she was directed to the medical ward, and as she walked down the long, empty corridor that reeked of antiseptic and boiled cabbage her heart was in her throat.

Arriving at the ward, she went in and approached the staff nurse in charge, who was sitting at the desk making notes. Two doctors were standing, their heads close together, conferring in hushed voices over a heart monitor. The sepulchral atmosphere made Lydia want to run.

Just then the nurse lifted her head and

her brow creased in a slight frown.

'Can I help you?'

Lydia shoved her hands in her coat pockets to stop them shaking, and nodded. 'I've come to see Sam Davenport. I understand he's in here.'

'Oh, yes, Dr Davenport. May I ask who you are?'

'Um—Lydia Moore.'

'Are you a relative, Miss Moore?'

'No, I—' She floundered. How could she describe her stormy and confused relationship with Sam? 'He's a friend—a neighbour. Is he all right? Can I see him?'

The nurse looked shocked at the very idea. 'It's rather late,' she explained, a little tersely. 'I'll just get the doctor to come and have a chat to you. Will you take a seat outside for a moment?'

She ushered Lydia out into the corridor where she paced aimlessly for a few minutes until one of the white-coated medics detached himself from the case-notes and made his way towards the door, kneading the bridge of his nose. He looked tired and irritable, and Lydia felt the universal rush of humility in the face of such selfless dedication. She had to remind herself sternly that he was no more qualified or dedicated than she was, and probably not much more tired.

'Miss—Moore, is it? I'm Mark Freeman, the SHO. I understand you're a neighbour of Dr Davenport.'

'Yes, Lydia Moore. I—Look, how is he?'

'I'm afraid I can't discuss his condition with you as you aren't a relative, and visiting has been over for some considerable time now.' His disapproval was almost physical, and Lydia felt herself crumble under the weight of it. Then she forced her head up and looked the doctor in the eye. Whatever his feelings, Sam needed her, and she intended to be there for him.

'I'm rather more than a neighbour, actually,' she bluffed, elasticising the truth. 'I—we live together. And I'm a doctor too.'

He sighed with relief. 'Well, why didn't you say so? Come on in and see him. He's driving everyone mad with his endless questions, all of which are pointless because he can't hear the answers at the moment, but he'll probably recognise you somehow. People do. We have all sorts of hidden senses that we don't realise we use.'

Lydia stopped his forward progress with a hand on his arm. 'Before we go in, could you tell me what's wrong with him? I don't know anything at all.'

He stopped and rubbed a hand over his face. 'Yes, of course. Look, let's get a coffee and I'll run over what we know.'

She followed him into the kitchen and he carried on talking to her over his shoulder. 'There was a fire at an agro-chemical plant, and some weedkiller apparently exploded—he was inside at the time, having just given first-aid to one of the employees, and the force of the blast blew the wall in and covered him in debris. Nothing broken, but the underneath of his forearms is pretty messy—grazes and some quite nasty bruising, that sort of thing. I imagine he flung his arms up to protect his face. Something obviously whacked him in the ribs, but otherwise the main damage seems to be his eyes. We bunged in some cyclopentolate drops to dilate his pupils, and we were able to get quite a good look inside his eyes with the slit-lamp microscope.'

'Any retinal detachment or other problems?' Lydia asked, struggling to keep her professional cool. She could hardly believe they were talking about Sam, *her* Sam. She blinked hard and tried to concentrate.

'No. The main damage seems to have been from flying debris. There were two tiny intra-corneal foreign bodies in his left eye, and we got them out with an eye-spud, and washed out about half a ton of rubble and grit from under the lids, but I don't think there'll be any permanent damage. Have a shot of caffeine.'

He handed her a mug, and she wrapped her hands around it gratefully. The doctor went on, 'We flooded his eyes with fluorescein so we could assess the damage. He's got fairly severe corneal abrasions in both eyes, but nothing much over the pupils, thank God. Damn sore, though, and his conjuctiva are scraped raw. They'll need dressing daily for a few days, and he'll have to have antibiotic ointment—can you do that for him?'

Lydia nodded. 'Of course.'

'Apart from that, he's gone totally deaf. Usual reaction to blast—tremendous roaring, blocking out all other sounds. The eardrums don't seem to have perforated, and hopefully again the damage is only temporary. I would expect that his hearing returns within the next few days at the most. Longer than that could indicate a permanent impairment.' He gave a slight, hollow laugh. 'Got a lousy temper, hasn't he?'

Lydia had to smile. 'Just a bit. Could I see him?'

'Sure. Bring your coffee—once he realises who you are, he probably won't let you go!'

She smiled, and he went on, 'He's frightened—people often are, under these circumstances. All he has left is touch, taste and smell, remember. Not much to help to orientate yourself, and he's fighting the sedation.'

'Typical,' Lydia said with a slight laugh, and followed the doctor into a small side-ward where a nurse was sitting by the bed, scanning a paperback. She stood up and crammed it into her pocket as they came in, greeting them quietly.

'How is he?'

'Not too bad now, Dr Freeman. Settling down at last. He's stopped asking questions, anyway. His TPR and blood-pressure are all quite normal, and he's passing urine OK.'

'Good. We're keeping him overnight

because he went into shock and his blood-pressure dropped quite severely, but he seems to have come out of it well.' He turned back to the nurse. 'This is Dr Moore, by the way. She's a close friend of Dr Davenport's. Has he had anything to drink?'

She shook her head. 'Nothing yet.'

'Mmm. We ought to start encouraging fluids—perhaps you'd like to have a go?' He turned to Lydia, and she lifted her shoulders in a helpless shrug.

'Sure. Whatever you say.' She was shocked by Sam's pallor, and the way he lay motionless on the bed, his restless energy stilled.

'You'll have to touch him. He doesn't know you're here.'

The doctor stepped out of the way, and Lydia moved up to the bed and got her first close look at him. His face was bruised and cut, his eyes lightly bandaged, and his mouth was set in a harsh, uncompromising line. His breathing was harsh and controlled, and he was obviously awake and fighting pain. She felt the hot sting of tears behind her eyelids.

Perching carefully on the edge of the

bed, she bent and brushed her lips against his hand, and he groaned and reached out for her, his hands grasping her arms in a desperate grip.

'Lydia?' he asked, his voice hoarse and strained. 'Thank God you're here.' His jaw clenched, and she could see the muscles working in his throat.

Lifting her hand, she smoothed the hair back from his face and kissed his brow lovingly. 'It's all right, darling,' she murmured, knowing he couldn't hear but unable to help herself. 'I'm here now. Just relax and try to sleep.'

She kept up the soothing movement of her thumb against his temple, and he turned his face into her hand and pressed his lips against her palm. 'I think I'm going mad,' he whispered. 'I can't see, I can't hear, and people keep doing things to me without any warning. I can't stand it. Get me out of here, for God's sake!'

Lydia slipped her arms around him and laid her head next to his, her cheek against his bruised and battered one, and let her love and reassurance flow into him. Gradually he relaxed, and after a few minutes she heard a gentle snore.

Easing her arms away from his shoulders,

she straightened and slid off the bed on to the chair, and rested her head against his hand, taking care not to lose contact with him for a second.

After an hour he woke briefly, confused and difficult, and she soothed him again and managed to get him to drink a little water. The nurse came in and out periodically, checking on him, and brought Lydia a cup of tea, which she drank without releasing Sam's hand.

'I'm glad you came,' the nurse said softly, 'he'd been asking for you for ages. We didn't know how to get hold of you, and he wasn't very coherent!'

'You surprise me,' she answered drily. 'He's usually vocally extremely explicit!'

The next time he woke was several hours later, at about four o'clock, and he was much calmer and more lucid; she guessed that the sedative had worn off. She had puzzled, while he was sleeping, on how to communicate with him, and had devised a simple 'one squeeze for yes, two for no and three for don't know' system. All she had to do was explain it to him!

In the event, it couldn't have been easier.

As he woke, he turned towards her,

squeezed her hand and said, 'Lydia?'

She squeezed back, once, firmly.

'Good,' he murmured, and shifted his weight a little. 'My eyes hurt—in fact, everything hurts,' he added, and she squeezed once, again.

'Did they get all the rubbish out of my eyes?' he asked, and she squeezed.

'Was that a yes?'

Squeeze.

'Thank God for someone with intelligence. Now maybe I'll get some answers.' He paused, and a muscle in his jaw worked for a second or two. 'Am I going to lose my sight?'

Two hard, emphatic squeezes, and his shoulders sagged in relief.

'What about my ears?'

Nothing. Lydia willed him to ask a question with a yes or no answer.

'Will I be deaf?'

Two squeezes, then a third, tentative.

'Maybe? Did my eardrums perforate?'

Two squeezes.

'Good,' he said, and thought for a moment. 'Can I go home now?'

Two squeezes.

'Why not?' he asked petulantly, and she smiled.

'You just can't, you difficult beast,' she couldn't resist saying, and he grinned.

'That was silly. I know you're talking to me, but I can't hear a damn thing. Why can't I go home? Because I'm not well enough, or because it's night-time?'

Two squeezes, but with a good long gap.

'Yes to both, eh?'

Squeeze.

'What's the time?'

She squeezed four times. There was a long pause, then he said heavily, 'I was frightened, Lydia. I don't think I've ever been so scared.'

Her hand tightened convulsively on his, and he pulled her towards him until she lay with her head against his chest. 'I was glad when you turned up. Please don't leave me alone. I need you, Lydia. Stay with me.'

She pressed her lips to the back of his hand, and his grip tightened almost painfully.

'You gave me such a fright,' she whispered, and, almost as if he could hear, his free hand came up and stroked her hair. Tears welled in her eyes and scalded down her cheeks, and she sniffed and wiped her cheek against the sheet.

'Are you crying?' he asked, his voice incredulous, and his fingers came up to trace the path of tears on her face. 'Ah, love, don't cry for me. I'm fine now you're here.'

His hands stroked her shoulders soothingly, and, comforted by his tender caress, she fell asleep, slumped against the edge of the bed, wrapped in his arms.

They were woken at six by the night staff doing the drugs.

Lydia straightened self-consciously, and the nurses gave her a sympathetic smile.

'You look shattered,' the young student said. 'I've been in and out doing his TPR and I don't think either of you noticed!'

'He's written up for pain-killers if he needs them. Do you think he does?' the staff nurse of the previous night asked.

Lydia shrugged. 'He's been sleeping all right, I think, but he was exhausted. He may feel worse once he wakes up. I'll ask him. May I?'

She borrowed a bottle of pills and, rousing Sam, she put the bottle in his hand, rattling it to show him what it was.

'Drug round?' he asked, and she squeezed his hand. 'Could I have some pain-killers?

My eyes are agony and my body feels as if it's been hit by a truck. I also need a pee, and I'm damned if I'm going to use that blasted bottle!'

'Alive and kicking,' Lydia said drily. 'Can I take him to the loo?'

'We've got a male nurse on the ward—I'll get him to help you,' the staff nurse said, and stuck her head round the door. 'Dave! Give us a minute, could you?' The young man joined them, and between them they got Sam to his feet and out to the bathroom. Lydia left Sam in the charge of the male nurse and took advantage of the brief respite to find the visitors' cloakroom in the corridor and freshen up herself. After a night bolt upright on a hard chair, with her head at an unnatural angle against Sam's chest, she felt pretty much run over by a truck, too.

She was also haunted by the slow, painful shuffle which was all he could manage. Gone was the Sam she knew, with the easy grace, the smooth, loose-limbed stride, the proud posture. In his place was a halting, fragile creature with only pride left between him and defeat, and she ached for him.

She told herself it was only temporary,

that by tomorrow he would be much more mobile and that she was being unnecessarily melodramatic, but she was tired—so tired, and her whole body yearned for rest. She splashed her face with cool water and combed the tangles out of her hair with her fingers, but she couldn't make much impression on her appearance without her handbag, and that was in Sam's room.

Wearily she made her way back and was surprised to see him sitting up in bed looking remarkably cheerful, with a cup of tea balanced at a precarious angle on his chest.

'He wouldn't have a feeder cup,' the ward orderly said with a laugh. 'Quite vocal, he was! I've put you a fresh cup on the side, dear.'

Lydia thanked her and rescued Sam's tea just as it began to dribble out of the side of the cup.

'Hey, I want that!' he yelled, and she put her finger on his lips, and then replaced it with her mouth.

'Good morning,' he said, much more quietly and with a slight lift to his mouth when she raised her head. 'Can I have my tea back now?'

She placed it carefully in his hands, and stood poised, ready to catch it again.

'For God's sake, stop hovering, woman! The worst I can do is spill it. Sit down and relax.'

So much for feeling sorry for him! Halting, fragile creature indeed! Tough as old boots and twice as indigestible. Dr Freeman was right about hidden senses. How had he known she was hovering?

She drank her tea, ignoring him when he slopped the contents of his cup on his bare chest above the opening of his hospital pyjamas.

'Damn,' he muttered, and reached out his hand. 'Can I have a tissue? And stop laughing at me, woman.'

'Stop calling me woman,' she bit back, slapping the tissue into his hand.

'Temper, temper!' he murmured, and Lydia could have hit him. She was discovering the frustration of trying to fight with someone who was intensely provocative, and far from oblivious to her reaction. He was, however, in an excellent position to ignore her. Shortly, she felt, she was going to kill him!

Their frustrating battle was brought to a halt by the arrival of Sam's breakfast.

'You may as well go home and get cleaned up,' the staff nurse said. 'The consultant will be round at nine, and I would think she'll say he can go home today, so if you could bring some clothes in to be on the safe side—the things he had on yesterday are filthy. Will you have time by nine?'

Lydia glanced at her watch, and saw that it was five-past seven.

'Probably,' she acknowledged. 'I'll have to arrange for a locum for today—I expect the neighbouring practice will be able to do the weekend, and I can take over from Monday.' She laughed. 'He's going to be hell to live with—I'll probably survive better if I'm busy!'

The staff nurse gave a commiserating smile, and Lydia stood up and kissed Sam, squeezing his hand.

'Are you going?' he asked, a note of panic in his voice, and Lydia smiled. All right to be independent so long as she was there, but when he thought she was leaving...! She squeezed his hand.

'You will come back?'

Squeeze, very firm and emphatic.

'Bye, then. See you later.' A hollow laugh at this, followed by a stream of curses as he dropped cold, soggy cornflakes down his chest.

Smothering a chuckle, Lydia left him, feeling much more cheerful and confident than she had an hour before. At least his tongue was all right!

By the time she had driven back to the village, showered and changed into clean jeans and a sweat-shirt, Mrs Mercer was letting herself into the surgery and opening the mail.

'Lydia! How is he, dear?' she asked, her normally cheery face creased with concern.

'Oh, he seems to be holding his own,' Lydia replied. 'No permanent damage, they don't think, and he looks OK apart from the bruises. His temper isn't improved by his predicament, though!'

Mrs Mercer smiled. 'Never is, is it, dear? Men can't take things like that the same way women do. My Bill always gets as mad as a hornet if he has to have a day off. Still, he's going to be all right, that's the main thing.'

She answered the phone, and while she was talking Lydia ran up to Sam's flat and found him some clean clothes, a razor and his toothbrush. Cramming them into

173

a plastic bag, she ran back down and checked her watch. Eight twenty-four.

'That was Dr Hastings, dear. He's arranged to cover for today by rescheduling his surgeries, and he says he'll do the weekend, but he wasn't sure what to do about next week. He thought you might want to do it, but he wasn't sure about Sam.'

Lydia stifled a pang of guilt. 'Could you ring George and tell him that I'll do it? It makes sense, doesn't it? If Sam doesn't like it he'll just have to lump it. That way I can be around for him, and the patients will get better care than they would from a stranger.'

'You don't have to convince me, dear,' Mrs Mercer replied. 'I think you should have had the job in the first place, but who am I to say? Just the tea-lady!' she sniffed.

Lydia hugged her. 'Bless you. Sam is a good doctor, and he's a fine man. He's just a little bigoted. You let me deal with him—and you are not to call yourself a tea-lady in my hearing again!'

She left then, and made it back to the hospital with three minutes to spare before the consultant arrived.

Sam was making a visible effort to contain himself when she arrived, but it was obvious that he was bored rigid and utterly frustrated by his absolute isolation from the world. His relief when he realised she was back in the room was almost physical, and she sat down on the now-familiar chair and held his hand, her thumb circling absently against the back, smoothing the fine, dark hairs that radiated down from his wrist.

'If you carry on doing that I won't be responsible for my behaviour,' he murmured, and Lydia snatched her hand away as if it were burnt.

His lazy chuckle greeted the slim, white-coated brunette who entered the room, and Lydia rose to meet her.

'Well, he sounds more cheerful,' she said, her voice crisp and businesslike. She held out her hand. 'Dr Moore, isn't it? I'm Mrs Wayne, the consultant in charge of Dr Davenport. I understand you'll be taking over his care when he returns home?'

'That's right,' she agreed, and the woman, who Lydia took to be in her late thirties, nodded.

'Good. Otherwise he'd have to come back every day to have the dressings changed and the ointment in, and that's less than desirable really. Right, well if you'd care to stay while I have a look at him I can talk you through the procedure and show you the damage as we go. Can I have the dressings trolley, please?'

She scanned the charts at the foot of the bed, and nodded her satisfaction. 'Nice and steady. I see he had a reasonable night.' She washed her hands in the basin near the door, and Lydia followed suit, more from habit than necessity.

'Right, let's have a look. His eyes are very badly scratched, and any infection could cause serious complications, so we're using chloramphenicol ointment. You'll have a job to see much, because he'll be severely photophobic and you'll have to work in dim light while you do the dressings.'

As she approached the bed she touched Sam's cheek with the back of her hand to warn him, and explained what she was going to do. 'Has he got any hearing back yet?' she asked the nurse, and she shook her head.

'Not that we know of. He hasn't said so, and I'm sure he would have done.'

Lydia choked down a laugh, and the

consultant raised a slim eyebrow at her. 'Like that, is it? OK! I'm just going to take off your bandages, Sam,' she said clearly, and began unwrapping the gauze. 'Someone close the curtains, please,' she murmured, and the light was cut down to a softer level. 'That's better.'

As the last strip of gauze was lifted away Lydia could see the extent of the damage. Sam's eyelids were swollen and bruised-looking, and his lashes were sticky with bloodstained secretions. 'Bathe his eyes, Nurse, please,' Mrs Wayne said as she pulled on sterile gloves, and Lydia had to watch as the girl gently stroked the secretions away with sterile cotton-wool.

Sam's mouth tightened, and Lydia gripped his hand firmly. She knew, and she realised that Sam knew, that the ordeal was hardly even started.

Once the secretions were cleared, the doctor gently but firmly lifted Sam's right eyelid and exposed the damage for Lydia to see. 'The fluorescein is still staining the abrasions—can you see the green stain on the cornea? This is the worst one, although the other eye had the debris buried in the cornea.'

Lydia nodded dumbly. Sam's hand had

tightened on hers almost unbearably, and she could see from the white line around his lips that he was in pain.

His eye was bloodshot and streaming, and he flinched when the thin strip of ointment was inserted under the lids. Mrs Wayne repeated the procedure with the other eye, finally stepping back and stripping off the gloves.

'Cover his eyes again, please, Nurse,' she said, and turned to Lydia. 'Think you can manage that?'

Lydia mumbled assent and struggled against a most unprofessional urge to cry. 'I'll save it for when he's been rude to me,' she joked, and the consultant smiled warmly at her.

'Not very nice, is it? But there we are, it has to be done. Nobody likes hurting a patient, but sometimes you have to be cruel to be kind. All you can do is be as quick and gentle as possible—but there, who am I to tell you that? You already know, I'm sure. Believe it or not, he's coming along nicely. I don't think there's any need to keep him in another night. Now, this is the ointment—chloramphenicol, and I'll get you some amethocaine drops just in case any other debris appears. I think we got it all out, but you never can be quite sure. I'll have some more sent up from the pharmacy before you go. If you can manage twice a day for the first couple of days, so much the better. The photophobia should wear off in a day or so as the corneas start to heal, but don't expect miracles. He'll still be jolly sore for several days.'

'When will he be able to work again?' Lydia asked, knowing it was one thing Sam was bound to want to know.

'Oh, not for at least a week, I wouldn't have thought. See how it goes, but certainly all of next week and maybe even the one following. Depends how stubborn he is.'

'As a mule,' Lydia said with a laugh, and the doctor chuckled.

'Usually are. Male doctors make the world's worst patients, without exception. Can you bring him in to see me in a week? I'll get Outpatients to send you an appointment.'

She left then, and after the nurses had gone Lydia turned to Sam and kissed him, as much for her own comfort as his.

'Have they gone?' he asked, and she pressed his fingers, more for reassurance than communication. 'God, that hurt. It's better now they've put in some more

179

ointment, but, hell's teeth, I didn't like it. Makes you think about the things we put patients through, doesn't it? I wonder when I can go home?'

Lydia picked up the bag of clothes, and emptied them on to his chest.

'Are these mine?' he asked, his face clearly delighted. 'Fantastic. I could do with a wash, I'm sure I must stink, but if I wait until I get home I can have a bath—'

She squeezed his hand twice, and he glowered at her—very effectively, considering he had lost his expressive eyes for the time being.

'What do you mean, no?' he said in a raised and aggravated voice. 'I want a bath, and I'll damn well have one!'

She squeezed his hand again, and he snatched it away. 'Don't go getting bossy, Lydia! You get stroppy with me, and I'll—'

She silenced him by the simple expedient of removing his clothes.

After a few moments of fulminating silence, he gave a wry chuckle. 'Like that, is it? I come quietly or not at all? Damn woman! Come here!'

He reached out his arms, and she went

willingly into them, hugging him fiercely.

'I love you, you difficult wretch,' she whispered into his hair, and then immediately wondered if he could, in fact, hear. Oh, so what? she thought. She really couldn't be bothered to hide her love for him any longer, so she said it again, and kissed him tenderly, just for good measure.

'Take me home,' he murmured against her lips, and she nodded.

Half an hour later they were on their way, and Sam's entry into the surgery was greeted with cries of delight by Mrs Mercer. Lydia led him up to his flat and persuaded him, without difficulty, to go to bed. Once there, he fell into a deep and untroubled sleep, and she used the time to make sure that George had everything he needed and to bring some of her clothes and bedding through to Sam's flat.

Stubborn and awkward though he might be, she had no intention of leaving him unattended for a minute until she was quite sure that he was all right. Like it or not, this was one woman doctor whom he was going to have to learn to trust...

181

CHAPTER EIGHT

Sam got his own way, of course. When he woke he needed the bathroom, so Lydia helped him in there and left him to it, praying that he would manage on his own, and hovering outside the door in case he didn't. She gave him a few seconds after the loo flushed, and then opened the door to see him perched on the edge of the bath, fumbling with the plug.

'What the hell are you doing?' she cried, and grabbed hold of him to pull him up and take him back to bed. She had forgotten his effortless strength, apparently undiminished by his ordeal.

He shrugged her off like a fly and carried on, eventually inserting the plug and then turning on the taps.

'No, Sam,' she wailed, tugging uselessly at him again, but he just grinned and carried on.

'As I see it,' he said, with a revolting attempt at humour, 'you can either leave me to fall and bash my head and drown, or you can help me. Either way, I'm having a bath. And no, a wash won't do,' he added as if he sensed her next impotent line of attack. 'I'm full of grit, my hair's sticky and matted, and I'm going to get clean.'

So saying, he stripped off his dressing-gown, turned off the taps and stepped cautiously into the water.

'Ah! Gorgeous,' he sighed, lying back in it and smiling contentedly. 'You still here?'

She stifled a chuckle and patted his intensely masculine knee with her hand. The texture was inviting, and she had to drag her hand away to stop it trailing unbidden over his lean hair-scattered thigh...

'Can't resist me, can you?' he said with a smirk, and she swallowed. Funny how his thoughts echoed hers so exactly. She smacked his leg, gently, and not even to herself would she admit that it was just an excuse to touch him again.

She flipped down the lid of the loo, settled herself on it and gave herself up to the luxury of admiring his superb but battered body. After a while he asked her to help him wash his hair, and, given the choice between watching him get shampoo

183

on the bandages and in his eyes or helping him, she slid down on to her knees and set to work.

He was right, of course. His hair was gritty and caked with dried blood, and in the process of massaging the shampoo into it she discovered myriad tiny bumps and bruises all over his scalp. The urge to caress was replaced by the urge to heal, and she turned her attention to his medical condition.

The bandage was getting soggy at the back, but he needed it changed anyway before long, and she planned to use a soft gauze pad held in place with micropore tape rather than a constricting band all round his head. She would deal with it once he was safely out of the water.

His hair finished, he insisted on standing up and scouring his body thoroughly from top to toe. She ran her eyes over him just as thoroughly, detecting all manner of cuts and scrapes and bruises—none serious enough to detract from his appeal. This time Lydia had to look away, because his effect on her was so overwhelming that she was sure he would detect it. For once, being a doctor conferred no immunity at all!

Once he was out, dried and safely covered up in bed again, Lydia dealt first with the cuts on his forearms, and then attended to his eyes, gritting her teeth before easing open his lids to squeeze in more ointment. She had to tell herself that the tears streaming down his cheeks were just involuntary watering caused by aggravation of the conjunctiva, not because he was crying with the pain, but she was having a hard time being dispassionate.

His gruff thanks were the last straw, and she went into the kitchen and made a good strong pot of tea while her nerves settled down again. Beautiful though his body was, it was scratched and battered from end to end. The bruise was coming out on his ribs, and the undersides of his forearms were cut to shreds. She had an almost overwhelming urge to take him in her arms and cuddle him better, and only a very serious word with herself prevented her from doing just exactly that.

He spent the rest of that day in bed, and she sat on a chair beside him, her bare feet propped against his side, reading while he dozed and grumbled alternately.

He was obviously bored to death and irritated beyond belief by the incessant roaring in his ears, and she dreaded the next few days until he regained either his sight or his hearing—and preferably both!

He was, in fact, surprisingly good about it. George popped up to see him at the end of surgery, and Judith brought him some flowers on Saturday morning.

'He may not be able to see or hear, but he can smell,' she said practically, and held the freesias under his nose.

'Gorgeous! I don't know who you are, but thank you. They smell wonderful.'

Lydia picked up his right hand and, taking his index finger, she wrote the letter J on the bed.

'J? Judith?' Lydia squeezed his hand. 'Judith, thank you.' He held out his arms, and Judith gave him an enthusiastic hug—reciprocated, Lydia noticed with a tiny twist of jealousy.

'Is he being good?' the nurse asked.

Lydia laughed. 'So-so. Considering what he's having to put up with, I would say he's being fantastic, but I'm beginning to get cabin fever.'

'Go out, then,' Judith suggested. 'I'll sit with him and make sure he doesn't do anything stupid. Go on, go. You can have till twelve—how's that?'

186

Lydia was doubtful, but the prospect of freedom was tempting. 'Are you sure...?'

'Out!' Judith said with a laugh, and Lydia nodded.

'OK.' She bent over Sam and kissed his cheek. Instantly his hand snaked out and grasped her wrist with unerring accuracy.

'Where are you going?'

Judith picked up his other hand and patted it reassuringly.

He sighed, and his head fell back against the pillow. 'Sorry, I'm being selfish. It didn't occur to me that you'd need to get out. I'll see you later.'

She wrapped up warmly and went out into the blustery March wind. It was sunny and bright, but the wind was keen and she turned her back to it and walked briskly down the lane, past the gravel pit which was the scene of David's daredevilry, and then on across the fields to Ron Blake's farm.

He was home now, and she saw him hobbling round his yard on crutches and went to say hello.

'I hear young Davenport's got himself in a mess at the weedkiller place,' he said.

Tom-tom drums, Lydia thought. 'Yes,

that's right. He'll be fine, though, in a few days.'

'Got you to look after him—can't be bad, lucky so-and-so. Things could be a lot worse for him!' He gave a hearty laugh, and Lydia joined in, trying furiously not to blush.

'How's the leg?' she asked, to change the emphasis.

'Oh, coming on, you know. Aches a lot, but I don't let it hold me up none. Can't, really. The missis can't do everything on her own, and we can't afford to pay a relief for too long. Still, mustn't complain. Could have been my neck, I s'pose!'

Lydia smiled and left him, following the footpath which ran down across the grassy field among the gentle heifers, then past the church to cut back into the village at the bottom of the hill near the shop.

Mrs Pritchard was standing near the window, and she waved to Lydia and indicated that she should come in. 'How is he, dear?' she asked, her kindly face worried.

'Oh, he's going to be fine,' she replied with a smile. You couldn't keep a secret ten seconds in the village.

'You give him our best—and here. Take

him these.' She handed over a bag of ripe, juicy peaches. 'Special treat. I know he likes them.'

'You must let me pay for them—' she began, but Mrs Pritchard cut her off with an indignant frown.

'Not on your Nellie, dear! He's carned them, every one. Sorted out my Peter's backache, he did, and we're right grateful. No, you give him those, love, with our blessing. And tell him to get better soon.'

Lydia purchased a few essentials to tide them over the weekend, and then, thanking Mrs Pritchard again, she made her way back up the hill.

Several people stopped her on the way to ask after Sam or pass on their regards, and by the time she reached her drive she was feeling quite choked by their warmth and love. They had felt this way about her grandfather, too, and many of them had said so today.

Letting herself in, she went quietly up to the flat and was surprised to hear rowdy laughter coming from the bedroom.

As she put away the shopping and undid her coat there was a long pause, followed by Sam's low rumbling voice, and Judith's quick, light laugh.

Lydia felt another twist of jealousy. How were they managing to communicate so well?

When she went into the bedroom Sam was slouched against the headboard, mumbling.

'Lettuce? No? Try light—no, we've had that. Limbo-dancer?'

'What on earth are you doing?' Lydia asked.

'Playing I-spy,' Judith answered.

'Lego?'

'His idea. I write a letter on the bed with his hand, and he then guesses it. Doesn't work the other way round, but he's bored enough to be silly.'

'Libido?' Sam suggested, and Judith laughed delightedly.

'See what I mean?'

'What is the answer?' she asked.

'Not libido? Pity. Try the next best thing—Lydia!' Sam guessed with a lazy smile, sitting up, and she moved forward and took his hand, trying unsuccessfully to fight down the blush. 'Hello, treasure,' he murmured huskily. 'I missed you. We've been playing I-spy. I think I've driven Judith crazy, actually. God, it's boring being in a padded cell.'

'Have you had a good time?' Judith asked, and Lydia nodded.

'Lovely. Went for a long walk and picked up some things in the shop. Everybody's been so nice about him—'

She stood up abruptly and turned away, her fraught emotions boiling over, and instantly Judith was at her side.

'Hey, come on, he'll be fine. It's just a bit of a shock—you love him, don't you?'

Lydia shushed her, with a panicky glance over her shoulder at Sam lying on the bed, but Judith shook her head.

'He still can't hear anything. Does he know?'

Lydia shook her head numbly. 'No. He has no idea. Oh, he knows I'm attracted to him, and he knows it's mutual, but he's fighting it every inch of the way. He doesn't want to get involved, and, like all men, he only allows himself to do what he thinks he should. If he doesn't want to fall for me, who am I to persuade him?'

'He's being pretty possessive—'

'Only because he's stranded. It won't last.'

'Lydia?' Sam's voice was full of concern. 'Is something wrong?'

She sat down again and squeezed his

191

hand reassuringly, then allowed him to pull her head down to his chest. 'I missed you,' he murmured against her hair, and she hugged him as hard as she dared.

'Liar,' she muttered. 'You were having a ball.'

In the background she heard the door close softly behind Judith, and she ached with despair. She loved him, and he was being so tender, so—so *approachable!* How on earth was she supposed to keep enough distance to maintain her sanity?

A tiny sob rose in her throat, and she turned it into a cough and stood up, putting some distance between them. Leaving his room, she went into the kitchen and put the kettle on, dashing aside the aggravating tears that got so persistently in the way.

Just as she had made the coffee she heard a crash in the bedroom, followed by a stream of curses that the merchant navy would have been proud of. Abandoning the drinks, she ran back to his room to find him stretched out full length on the floor, clutching his shin.

Shaking her head, she helped him to his feet, scolding him all the while and trying not to let her trembling hands betray her. She might have saved her breath.

'Stop telling me off,' he muttered, and limped back to the bed, gingerly exploring his bruised shin. 'And why are you shaking? Did I frighten you? I was coming to find you—I know there's something wrong, and I was worried. Don't be mad with me, Lydia.'

He grinned sheepishly, and she dropped to her knees and kissed his shin better, then thrust his jeans into his hand. The sooner that beautiful body was covered up, the better she was going to be able to cope!

He pulled on the jeans, then the sweatshirt, and held out his hand. She took it, and he shook his head impatiently.

'Socks and shoes,' he said. 'I could do with some fresh air.'

She found some and handed them to him, and then took him into the sitting-room and gave him his coffee before leading him down the stairs and out into the garden.

'Oh, marvellous,' he said with obvious pleasure. 'I can feel the wind, and smell the wet leaves and the grass—is someone mowing their lawn? What an incredibly evocative smell. I think spring has sprung!'

Shoulder to shoulder, hip to hip, with their

arms wrapped round each other's waists, they walked down the path to the end. Reaching out, Lydia picked a leaf and crushed it under his nose.

'Bay,' he said promptly, and breathed in deeply. 'God, it's good to be alive.'

Lydia had to agree. They spent nearly an hour in the garden, with Sam soaking up the scents and enjoying the feel of the wind tugging his hair and playing over his face, and then she took him back up to the flat and curled up with him on the sofa and fed him ham sandwiches and thick wedges of juicy peach, washed down with fruit juice and followed with more coffee.

He dozed after that, and later on they sat holding hands while Lydia read a book. She cooked chicken supreme and rice for supper, so that he could manage it easily with a spoon, and then she helped him bath before doing his eyes again.

Deciding to leave that chore until she had bathed herself, she left him in front of the fire and forced herself to hurry.

Not fast enough, though, because by the time she came out he was in the kitchen finding himself a drink of water, and the rug from the sofa was lying where he had dropped it, one end draped over

194

the fire-guard and just starting to burn.

Snatching the glass from him, she hooked the blanket away from the fire and doused the flames, then, seizing him by the hand, she led him to the fire, held his hand out to it, and put the soggy blanket in his hand.

'Oh, my God,' he whispered. 'Did I drop the blanket in the fire?'

'Yes, you damn well did, you silly fool! Why can't you stay where you're put? You'll be the death of us both if you go on like this! Bed!' She marched him firmly into the bedroom, and pushed him down on to the edge of the bed, then swung his legs up so that he had no alternative but to lie down.

Switching off the bedroom light, she washed her hands and stripped off the tape holding the dressing over his eyes with unsympathetic speed.

'Ouch!' he yelled, and she glared at him.

'I'll give you ouch, you maniac! Lie still!'

She eased the pads away from his eyes, and was relieved to see that the oozing seemed to have stopped. As she reached for the ointment Sam's lean fingers circled her wrist and she turned back, to see his bloodshot, watering eyes fixed unwaveringly on her face.

'I love you,' he said softly, and her face crumpled.

'I love you, too,' she whispered, and he pulled her down and kissed her with great tenderness.

'Don't cry, darling,' he murmured. 'Do my eyes and then come to bed. I need to hold you. For two days I've been sitting in a vacuum with nothing to do but think, and I can't fight this any more.' His voice was ragged with emotion, and his poor, damaged eyes blazed with shattering intensity. 'I need you. Sort my eyes out quickly and come here...'

Her hands were trembling so much that she could hardly hold the ointment, and Sam took it from her and put it in himself, then closed his eyes gratefully and allowed her to cover them.

As soon as she was finished he stood up and stripped off his dressing-gown, and then reached for her, easing her nightdress over her head. Ridiculously, she was shy, but he seemed to understand and wrapped her in his arms, holding her gently against his warm body. The fire and urgency of a moment before was gone, replaced with a devastating tenderness.

'Trust me,' he whispered against her hair. 'This is between us. Every breath, every touch, every word—it's just for us. We have to trust—I'll never hurt you. I love you.'

Slowly, as if released from a trance, Lydia lifted her arms and circled his waist, hugging him hard against her. 'I love you, too,' she said, her lips against his skin, and, as if he understood, a shudder ran through him. He released her and moved towards the bed, getting in and holding the quilt open for her so that she could slide in beside him, then he wrapped it around her and lay against her, face to face, her breasts pressed against the soft curls that covered his broad chest, one of his legs thrown possessively over hers, cradling her against his hips.

She could feel that he wanted her, feel the hard jut of his masculinity against the soft curve of her hip, but he made no move to touch her, apparently content for now to hold her and let her relax in the circle of his arms.

Confused, she lifted her hand and placed it against his cheek, and he turned his face into her palm and kissed it gently.

'Go to sleep,' he murmured, and to her surprise she felt her lashes drifting down over her eyes as she slid into blissful oblivion.

She woke in the night to one of those strange spells of absolute clarity, to find his legs still entwined with hers, although he had rolled on to his back and one arm was flung above his head. She felt cocooned in a delicious warmth, surrounded by his love, and, although they had yet to make love, she knew their capitulation was complete. Whatever happened now, it could not deepen her love for him.

What was certain, however, was that, short of famine, flood or earthquake, they were going to make love, and probably before dawn.

Sanity reared its head and she carefully disentangled her legs from his and eased herself away from him, standing up and tugging on his dressing-gown as she headed for the door.

She crept downstairs and let herself into the dispensary, where she raided a drawer with lightning speed and ran quickly back upstairs again, pocketing the keys.

She was too slow—or perhaps he was just so closely in tune with her, because she found Sam standing in the bedroom doorway, a puzzled frown on his face. He must have felt the floor move as she walked towards him, because he held out his arms and drew her into them.

'Where did you go? I missed you.'

She took his hand and placed her spoils in it, and he closed his fingers around the booty with another puzzled frown. 'What? Ah. Good girl. However many did you get?' He counted, passing the little packets from hand to hand. 'Eight-*eight*? Are we going for a record?' Laughter touched his voice, and she flushed awkwardly. She hadn't thought of numbers, merely of the fact that someone had better take some precautions.

She moved away from him, embarrassment heating her cheeks. She had never done this before, didn't know where to begin or how to be sophisticated.

'Lydia?'

The laughter was gone from his voice now, replaced with tenderness and something else—something urgent that called to her body while her mind was still reeling with shame.

'Lydia, come here.'

Even as he voiced the soft command, she was moving towards him, the dressing-gown somehow sliding from her shoulders so that by the time she reached him they were both as nature had intended.

This time as his arms closed around her her body was ready for his, and the fierce beat of arousal throbbed in her veins.

He eased her down, trembling, to the bed, and as he came down beside her his lips found hers with unerring accuracy.

She hadn't realised that passion could spiral quite so high and quite so fast, but before she knew what was happening she was clinging to him, running her hands feverishly over his back, his shoulders, biting and soothing, stroking and caressing. His skin felt like living silk to her untutored hands, and she revelled in the texture, oblivious to his fevered response. She could hear her voice begging, pleading for something—some unknown touch or magic word that would bring release, and she could have screamed with frustration and disbelief when he moved away from her.

Within seconds he was back, soothing her with his hands, rekindling the flame to fever pitch, and then with one smooth, swift stroke she was bound to him forever and the world exploded in an endless cacophony of sensation.

She clung to him, anchored to him in sheer desperation as she fought against the magic he wrought, but then his voice found her in the darkness, his words harsh and pleading, and she was lost.

'Now, darling, please, now—*yes!*'

As his primeval cry rent the air the world exploded all around her, leaving her stripped bare of all she had ever known, and within it all was a deep stillness, a true communion with him deeper than mere mortals could begin to understand. As she gave herself to him utterly, so it seemed to her that she took the gift of his soul in return.

Gradually the awful trembling ceased, and she lay quiet in his arms, stunned by the awesome majesty of the moment.

'I love you,' he said quietly, with great sincerity, and then the tears started to fall, huge, heavy tears that rolled faster and faster down her cheeks until her hair was drenched and her throat was raw; then he cradled her close and kissed her firmly.

'Enough now,' he murmured. 'Go to sleep. We'll talk later.'

'I didn't know,' she whispered, 'I had no idea. I love you...'

Gradually her grip relaxed and she faded into sleep, safe in the circle of his arms.

Sunday morning was much like any other cold, bright morning, but to Lydia it would always have a splendid memory.

Sam woke her with a touch so soft that it was little more than a sigh, and the brush of his lips stirred her to wakeful awareness. As memory returned she felt a twinge of embarrassed shyness which his gentle persistence soon dispelled, leaving in its wake a light-hearted wantonness which seemed to delight him.

They made love without hurry, revelling in the touch and taste and smell which were all Sam had at his disposal. For Lydia, of course, there was the added bonus of sight and sound, and she stared unashamedly at his magnificent body, delighting in his hoarse cries and ragged breathing as she tormented him with her touch.

Although the beginning lacked the fevered haste and utter desperation of the first time, the pace soon quickened, overtaking the first experience and hurling them headlong into unimagined ecstasy.

Afterwards Sam rolled on to his side, taking her with him, and sighed with disbelief.

'Wow!' he murmured when he could speak. 'That was...I'm speechless. You're amazing!'

Lydia laughed softly and snuggled up to him. Now that they belonged to each other, now that the gifts had been given and received, their coming together was sheer joy, the terror of the unknown lost forever in the safety of his embrace. This was where she belonged, and nothing and no one could ever destroy their happiness.

Monday came all too soon, with the demands of the practice taking precedence over Sam, at least physically, if not spiritually.

Technically speaking, she was in the surgery dealing with the usual post-weekend rush of sore throats and tummy-troubles, but her ears were strained for the sound of Sam in the flat above her; hopefully his mishaps of Saturday would have warned him, but just to be on the safe side Mrs Mercer popped up at nine-thirty after the phone stopped its first frantic burst, and Judith took her coffee break with him at ten-fifteen after her surgery.

It was eleven-thirty before Lydia finished with the last patient, and she then had to sit and sign a whole pile of repeat prescriptions for collection after midday before she could snatch ten minutes with him.

He was up and dressed, sitting on the sofa with a lost look on his face when she went up. He pulled her on to his lap and kissed her gently, then laid his head against her breasts and sighed.

'I miss you. I know life has to go on, but yesterday was so beautiful. I wish you could get another locum so you could be with me, but that's just selfish, isn't it? Anyway, as you've pointed out to me on countless occasions, you are the best person to take over.'

She kissed him in gratitude for that. She had been so worried about how he would take it, and to know that she had his backing was a huge relief. She made them both a cup of coffee and stayed with him while he drank it, then reluctantly kissed him goodbye and went back to her duties.

She had three calls to make, one to Ida Humphreys, who was making good progress after her pulmonary embolus, one to a pregnant woman who was suffering from high blood-pressure and refused to go into hospital—Lydia couldn't blame her, but she was nevertheless concerned—and the third was to David Leeming's grandmother, who was suffering from a bad bout of bronchitis.

After reassuring her that she would be all right, and prescribing antibiotics to clear up the infection, Lydia had a chat to Mrs Leeming about David, who was doing much better at school.

'I had a word with Billy James's mother, and apparently Billy is very unhappy and misses his father,' Mrs Leeming explained. 'Still, he'll be out of prison soon and then Billy may get back to normal. We had him to tea,' she added, 'and they seemed to get on rather well. Perhaps that's the answer! Oh, and I had a phone call from Jack Torrence—he's going to be up this way next weekend and wants to take me out for a meal. Do you think I should go?'

Goodness, Lydia thought, she can't be any older than me, and she's been widowed and has a son of five. What have I done all my life? The young woman's face was troubled, and Lydia wondered what to say. 'Do you want to go?' she asked eventually.

'Yes, I think I do. I just didn't want to upset David now he's settling down so nicely, but—I don't know, I can't live my life for him forever, and Jack... Who knows? It may all come to nothing, but it would be nice...' She trailed off, looking a little awkward, and Lydia smiled reassuringly at her.

'Wait and see. But go, definitely. Give yourself a chance. You never know, it could turn into the love-affair of the century!'

Mrs Leeming blushed and laughed. 'Oh, I doubt it, but it might be fun—still, I mustn't hold you up. Thank you for calling on Mum.'

'Pleasure,' Lydia said, and made her way back to the surgery, humming softly as she drove. Was it because she was so much in love with Sam that she wanted the rest of the world to be happy too? She realised she was smiling. Ridiculous! Her smile broadened to a grin, then to a laugh of sheer delight. It really didn't matter. She had a right to hum, to laugh, to smile, to sing—the world was a wonderful place, and she was glad to be alive.

The rest of the day passed in a blur. Her antenatal clinic was due to start at three, but just as she was about to go up and have lunch with Sam at one-thirty the phone rang. Mr Gooch had had another heart attack, and Lydia snatched up her bag and went out again. After she had examined him, given him an injection of morphine to dull the pain and set up the portable oxygen, she called the ambulance and stayed with him, trying to calm his distressed wife.

'Will he die this time?' she asked tearfully.

Lydia could only be honest. 'Let's hope not, but another attack so soon after the first isn't a good sign. The most important thing at the moment is to get him into hospital so that they can monitor him closely. The next forty-eight hours will be the most critical. If you take some things with you you should be able to stay at the hospital with him.'

The ambulance arrived soon afterwards, and Lydia saw the drowsy patient and his wife off before returning to the surgery. It was ten-past three, and she apologised to her waiting mums and started the antenatal

207

clinic without stopping for lunch.

Mrs Mercer brought her in a cup of tea and told her that Sam wanted a word, but she didn't have time to go up.

'Could you keep an eye on him for me, Mrs Mercer? I can't get away just now, but I'll try and go up before surgery.'

In the event the clinic overran and she went straight on, switching from pregnancy to tonsillitis with practised ease.

Finally, at seven o'clock, the last patient went home, and Lydia was just on her way up to see Sam for the first time since the morning when Sir James popped his head round the door.

'Hello, young lady! How're you doing?'

'Sir James! Fine. I was just going to lock up—come on in. How nice to see you. Come through to the house—Sam's resting upstairs and I don't want to disturb him.'

In truth, she worried about how to cut off Sam's affectionate greeting in front of an audience! Because she had no doubt that he would be affectionate at the very least, if not downright passionate!

She led Sir James through to the newly decorated sitting-room, and poured him the usual brandy, fixing herself a small sherry. She didn't usually drink on an empty stomach, but tonight she felt she had earned it.

'So, tell me all about Sam,' Sir James began, settling himself in the settee. 'How's he managing?'

'Oh, well, he seems to be doing OK. He's terribly independent—does exactly as he pleases and to hell with the consequences. He's finding it very lonely, though, and he's totally isolated, of course. He's nearly impossible to communicate with, and he's so pig-headed! It wouldn't be so bad if he would accept help, but no, he ploughs ahead regardless, because he knows best, and so he makes mistakes—'

'Mistakes?'

'Silly, potentially harmful little blunders. Nothing to get excited about yet, but give him time and we could have a real tragedy on our hands. I've tried so hard not to interfere, but it's very difficult to stand back and let things take their course. If he would only accept that he can't cope alone—still. That's Sam for you.'

Sir James eyed her kindly. 'Forgive me, my dear,' he said, very quietly and gently in a way that reminded her painfully of her grandfather, 'I don't want to intrude, but do you have a personal interest in this

209

rather headstrong young man?'

Her face softened, and her voice became slightly husky. 'Yes. Yes, I do. I'm afraid he's come to mean rather a lot to me, Sir James.'

He smiled. 'You could do a great deal worse, young lady. Tell me, how's our young friend Miss Parkins?'

'Oh, Susie.' Lydia rubbed her eyes tiredly. 'Grim. Sam just can't seem to get to the bottom of it. There must be something we've missed, but it's so difficult. There's nothing that's obviously wrong, but she's going downhill fast. I just feel so impotent to help her, and Sam—Sam's no help at all!'

'I'm sure you'll make certain that everything possible is being done for her in Sam's absence.'

Lydia sighed. 'I'll try. I've discussed her with Sam at length; we often talk about cases we're handling and I wish I could discuss this one with him now, but at the moment I can't get through to him.'

'Do you think you could work together?'

'In partnership? I'd love it, but I'm not so sure about Sam. He doesn't want to work with a woman again, and I wouldn't dare suggest it!'

'Too distracting, eh?'

She laughed and blushed, and he patted her on the shoulder as he rose to leave.

'I'd like to see you two in partnership, you know—one way or the other. And I know your grandfather would. He worried about you.'

'There was no need—and as for my partnership with Sam, I'm working on it. By the time I've finished with him I will have made myself so indispensable that he won't know how he managed without me!'

He leant towards her. 'Professionally or personally?' he asked with a wink.

'What do you think?' she said with a laugh.

'I think I'll wish you luck, my dear. I have a feeling you'll need it.'

She laughed. 'Thank you, Sir James.'

She showed him to the door, and as she closed it she turned to see Sam standing in the hall behind her.

'Oh! You made me jump! What on earth are you doing down here?' She moved towards him, but then something about his stillness halted her progress and she trailed to a stop. 'Sam?'

'Why was Sir James here?'

'He came—you can hear—!'

'Answer the question, Lydia.' His voice was like ice, and dread slithered down her spine.

'He came to see how you were doing.' Her voice was puzzled, and tinged with guilt. How much had he heard?

'Are you sure? Are you certain he didn't come to find out how your little scheme was progressing?'

She gasped. 'What little scheme?'

His mouth hardened into a thin, bitter line. 'The one to make yourself so indispensable to me that I won't know how I managed without you...the one to trap me into taking you on as a partner—that little scheme!'

CHAPTER NINE

Lydia was stunned. He had heard—but oh, how he had misheard! She reached for him, desperate to make him understand.

'Darling, I—'

'Don't darling me!' he yelled, snatching his arm away. 'My God, to think I trusted you! All those lies—' His chest heaved, and his mouth was taut with rage. Hot flags of anger blazed on his cheeks, and she could almost feel the searing contempt of his gaze through the layers of gauze.

'You don't understand,' she wept, and he drew back as though she were something vile.

'Don't give me that rubbish. For God's sake, don't lie to me any more! You've said enough—I should have been warned! You're like every other lying whore—sleeping your way into the practice when everything else has failed, making yourself indispensable—!'

She flinched at the contemptuous venom in his voice, but the worst thing was hearing her own words flung back at her. Oh, yes, she could see how he had read them, but he was wrong—so wrong. If only she could explain...

'Sam, you're making a mistake—'

'No! The only mistake I've made is to trust you. You're fond of accusing me of that, aren't you? I couldn't believe my ears when I heard you telling Sir James about all these so-called mistakes I've made—what the hell are you trying to do? Discredit me? Get me struck off with your evil little lies so that you can have the practice? Thank God your grandfather isn't alive to see this. He worshipped you, did you know that? Well, you're down off his damn pedestal now, you scheming little bitch.'

Hurt and outraged, she launched her only defence—attack. 'You can talk!' she yelled. 'Conniving and manipulating my grandfather into leaving you the practice premises—you can talk about making yourself indispensable and wheedling your evil way into someone's affections! I suppose you were hoping to persuade me to marry you so that you could get the rest of the house! Well, tough! I wouldn't marry you if you were the last man on earth. You don't even know what love is. You're so bitter and twisted, so busy being endlessly self-sacrificing and nursing all these imagined wrongs that you can't see love when it hits you in the face! Well, I don't need that, Dr Davenport. I don't need *you*, and I certainly don't *want* you,' she sobbed, her voice breaking on the lie.

She whirled away, her only thought escape, but he was too quick for her, seizing her arm and dragging her up against his body.

'You're lying again,' he muttered savagely, knotting his hands in her hair and yanking her head back. 'You do need me, the way a fish needs water. Like every other scheming woman, you'll use that need to further your own ends—well, fine. You hold yourself so cheaply that who am I to turn you down? We'll see who wants who—' His mouth ground down on hers, bruising the lips which so recently had yearned for his touch, and his free hand dragged her against his body, making her achingly aware of his passionate response.

Gradually the kiss changed, no more gentle but yet giving as well as taking, driving her to a fever pitch that overruled her objections and stifled her protest at birth.

With a low moan of anguish she melted against him and he gentled her for a moment, then with a superhuman effort he wrenched himself away from her.

'You see,' he rasped, 'you do want me. And you make me want you—damn you.'

'Go to hell!' she sobbed.

'I'm already there,' he said bitterly, his voice raw with pain and disillusion. Then with a shuddering sigh he turned and groped his way slowly, cautiously back along the hall and through the door to the surgery.

Shaken and trembling, Lydia ran up the stairs and through the door on the landing, arriving in the flat before him. She was in the bedroom snatching up her scattered possessions when he came in, his face a cold mask.

'What are you doing?'

'Getting my things,' she bit back, and tried to move past him, but he refused to shift, his hands gripping her arms, and she could feel him trembling.

'Why?' he asked, his mask cracking.

'Oh, Sam,' she whispered, and he wrapped his arms around her, hugging her fiercely.

'I really thought we had something—'

He tipped up her chin and his lips sought her mouth, fierce and demanding, and she met his passion with a need of her own, equally fierce, equally demanding.

Somehow their clothes were stripped aside and they fell tangled on the bed, their bodies urgent with desire, all reason banished. Sam was rough, but she was rougher, fighting desperately for her life— for her love. With a wild cry they tumbled over the edge, clasped in each other's arms, words of love and hate mingled with their tears.

Then he rolled away from her, his face expressionless.

'Get out,' he said, his voice devoid of emotion.

Shaking uncontrollably, Lydia stood up, gathered her things together and moved to the door. 'What about your eyes?' she asked through stiff lips.

'What about them? Judith can do them in the morning. I don't want you in my practice, either. I'll be down first thing, and Mrs Mercer can contact another locum. George can cover until someone can get here. I don't want to see you or speak to you again.'

Numbly she stumbled through to the house, locking the door behind her in a futile gesture of self-defence.

She made it to the bathroom, just, before her body rebelled and she was suddenly, violently sick.

She was woken by Judith, shaking her shoulder and peering at her with troubled eyes.

'Lydia? What's happened? Sam's in the

surgery creating havoc, demanding another locum, and going mad because there isn't anyone available at the moment. He's reduced Mrs Mercer to tears, and now he's torn the bandages off his eyes and said he'll do the surgery himself. It's absolute bedlam, and the patients are due to arrive any minute. He can't see, his eyes are streaming constantly and he can't bear the light on—there's no way he can do the surgery, but I can't persuade him. You've got to come and help.'

'No.' She turned over, but Judith dragged her back.

'You have to!'

'I don't!' Lydia cried. 'I don't have to do anything for him—and don't you maul me, too!'

Judith's hand dropped to her side, and her eyes widened in disbelief. 'Lydia? What happened?'

She shook her head. 'Nothing. Nothing you need worry about. We just—he—Oh, damn!'

She fumbled under her pillow for a soggy tissue, and scrubbed fiercely at her eyes. 'Make me a coffee, and I'll get up and do his damn surgery. Give me a minute to get him upstairs, and you can let the patients in and tell them I've been out on a call.'

She threw back the bedclothes and ignored Judith's sharply indrawn breath. So her body was bruised—it was nothing compared to her heart.

'What did he do to you?' she asked in horror.

'I fell up the stairs,' Lydia lied.

'In other words, mind your own business, Judith.' The nurse turned and walked to the door. 'I'll put the kettle on while you get rid of Sam.'

That was easier said than done. He looked awful, standing in the dispensary with his back to the light, his eyes streaming, hardly able to open them.

'What are you doing?' she asked furiously.

'Looking for the amethocaine drops,' he snapped. 'What the hell are you doing? I told you not to come in here—'

'You can't work like this! Look at you! You'll get an infection in your eyes and then you'll go blind—much as I think you probably deserve it, I can't let you do that. Get out of here—go on, go upstairs and let Judith dress them, and let me get on with the surgery—'

'*No!*' he roared.

'Yes,' she replied firmly. 'You have a duty to your patients, and, whatever misconceptions you might have about my personal and moral behaviour, you know damn well that I'm a good doctor. Now go away. I'll do my best to get a replacement as soon as possible, if you insist, but you are doing nothing this morning. Savvy? Nothing.'

His shoulders drooped in defeat, and his eyelids closed painfully slowly. 'OK. But only because I have no choice,' he said flatly.

'Judith, take him away and look after him, would you?' she asked, her voice surprisingly level.

Mrs Mercer brought in the patients' notes and a cup of coffee, and patted Lydia on the shoulder without saying a word.

The morning seemed endless. She avoided her patients' curious eyes, dealt with them as briskly as possible and went out on the calls after signing a pile of scrips and sipping half-heartedly at her coffee. She came back and picked at the sandwich Judith put in front of her, then dictated some letters to Mrs Mercer and glanced through the post.

There was a letter from the FHSA addressed to Sam, which she put on one side and then read at the end, despite her intention not to do so. In the event she was glad she did.

Dear Dr Davenport, It has become apparent that both your practice and that of Dr Hastings are running at full stretch, and it would seem desirable to form some sort of more permanent link between the two practices. In view of the steady expansion of light industry in the area, the possibility of setting up a small health centre to serve the four villages and outlying areas has been considered. Under the circumstances, were you and Dr Hastings to form a partnership, the FHSA would be willing to fund the development of such a health centre and would also fund the appointment of an additional partner for the joint practice.

On that subject, it has been brought to our attention that Dr Lydia Moore, who, as you may know, was related to your predecessor, is now living in the area and is looking for a permanent appointment. We understand that she has in fact worked in your practice as a locum in recent weeks, and as she knows the area she would seem an ideal choice.

The position would, of course, have to be advertised, and is only hypothetical at the moment, pending a decision on the development of the health centre. Perhaps you could discuss it with Dr Hastings and come back to me? I look forward to your comments on the matter. Yours, et cetera.

Lydia dropped the letter on to the desk. Damn. What timing! She glanced at the date, and saw that it had been written on Friday, long before— She closed her eyes. The highs and lows of the last three days were too heart-wrenching to contemplate. She shoved the letter into a drawer, and went through to her part of the house to wash and freshen up before the evening surgery.

The next two days passed. That was all that could be said for them, and the nights were infinitely worse. Whenever she was alone Lydia found herself going over their row again and again, and as the days went by it seemed more and more unreal.

She gathered from Judith that Sam's eyes were healing well. He had an appointment with the ophthalmic surgeon on Friday morning, and took himself in a taxi. Lydia caught her first glimpse of him since Tuesday morning, and she was shocked at the change in him. He looked thin and drawn, his face bleak, and his shoulders were stiff with pride. She wanted to cry.

After surgery and repeat scrips Lydia picked up her list of house calls and scanned them listlessly. One name caught her eye, and her heart sank. Susie Parkins.

Picking up her bag, she made her way out to the car just as Sam arrived back. She noticed that his eyes were uncovered, but he was wearing dark glasses. Hesitantly, her heart pounding, she made her way over to him.

'Sam?'

He stiffened and turned to her. 'Did you want something?' he asked coldly.

She swallowed. 'I have to go on a call—Susie Parkins. She's jaundiced, apparently, and in pain. I wondered...'

He sighed. 'What do you want me to do about it?'

'Come with me? I know it's not very orthodox, but—'

'I'll come,' he said crisply, and followed her back to the car. 'So what do you know?' he asked, once they were settled.

'Only what I've told you. I didn't take the message.'

'Why did you want me to come?' he asked bleakly, and she realised that he was finding this as difficult as she was.

'You didn't have to,' she snapped, and then sighed as she pulled up outside the Parkinses' house. 'I'm sorry. I just wanted you here for another opinion. Two heads, and all that. It just sounds all rather serious now.'

He nodded. 'It does, doesn't it? Will you admit her? I think it's time.'

'I hoped you'd say that. I think we've come to the limit of what we can do here. She saw the consultant at the beginning of the week and had an abdominal ultrasound, sigmoidoscopy and barium enema. All normal. We've ruled out all the obvious, easy answers, haven't we?'

Their eyes met. 'I'm afraid so,' he said heavily, and his hand reached out to hers. The contact brought all her feelings to the surface with a rush, and she was sure her longing must be written on her forehead in letters ten feet high.

'Oh, Sam,' she whispered, and he snatched his hand away and opened the door.

'Come on. Let's go and find out the situation.'

It was every bit as bad as they had feared. Susie was pale, her skin tinged with the faint yellow of slight jaundice, and she had severe upper-abdominal pain with marked epigastric tenderness. She gripped Sam's hand and looked pleadingly into his eyes.

'I'm not making it up, Dr Davenport,' she said weakly.

He squeezed her hand. 'I know you aren't, Susie. I never thought you were.'

'Will I have to go to hospital?' she asked, and he nodded.

'Yes, I think you should. I think they need to have a look inside and see what's wrong, love. Mrs Parkins, would you sort her out some night-clothes and wash things, please? Dr Moore, perhaps you could call an ambulance and arrange for her admission.'

'I'm going to die, aren't I?'

Lydia froze in her tracks, Mrs Parkins clapped her hand over her mouth and choked down a sob, and Sam paused almost imperceptibly before producing a heart-warming, reassuring smile.

'Whatever gave you that idea?' he said gently. 'You just need an operation to find out what's wrong inside—'

'Truly?'

'Truly.' He smoothed back the hair from her damp forehead with a gentle hand. 'Once they've found out what's wrong with you, then we'll know what to do to make you well again. In the meantime you just rest as much as you can.'

'Dr Davenport?'

'Yes, Susie?'

'Thank you for believing me,' she whispered, too quietly for her mother to hear, and Sam smiled, patted her hand and went to stand by the window.

Lydia called the hospital, spoke to the surgical registrar on take and arranged for Susie's admission, all the time staring at the wall and seeing Sam's smile. When the arrangements were made Lydia put the phone back on the cradle and turned to Mrs Parkins brightly.

'The ambulance will soon be here, and then they'll get her sorted out.'

'Will she—I mean...?'

Lydia led the woman into another room

and laid a comforting arm around her shoulders. 'She's very ill. It looks as though her pancreas is giving up, for some reason. They need to operate to sort her out, but the surgeon will discuss it with you once you arrive. I don't want to tell you one thing for him to confuse you with another, so it's best to wait and see him. He's got all the results of the tests, anyway, so he knows as much as we do. Just try and be strong for Susie, because she's obviously not at all well and she needs to be able to lean on you.'

Mrs Parkins nodded. 'I'm sorry I was so nasty about you,' she blurted out. 'I was just worried.'

'It's all right,' Lydia soothed. 'I do understand. Love makes us do all sorts of strange things.'

The ambulance arrived then, much to everyone's relief, and Sam and Lydia stood on the drive, watching it leave with a sense of defeat.

'What do you think?' she asked.

'Cancer of the pancreas—as you suggested? I hope to God I'm wrong, but I don't think so. If it's any comfort to you, you suggested that last week and I thought you were wrong—'

'Why the hell should that be any comfort to me?' she cried, and, to her horror, she burst into tears. Sam left her to it for a minute, then thrust a clean hanky into her hands.

'Come on,' he said wearily, 'let's get back.'

'What did Mrs Wayne say about your eyes?' Lydia asked once they were on their way.

'Progressing well, and I can go back to work on Monday. Can you cover the weekend?'

She nodded. 'Sure. Don't you mind?'

'Do I have a choice?' he asked bitterly. 'And, as you pointed out yourself, whatever I think of your morals, you're a good doctor.'

It was a busy weekend, and in a way Lydia was glad to hand over to Sam because she was finding it impossible to cope.

On the other hand, once she had nothing to occupy her mind, her misery over Sam intensified until she could think of nothing else. She tackled the long-overdue dining-room with very little enthusiasm, and ended up blowing a fortnight's salary paying a firm to come in and finish it and decorate the hall while she dug listlessly in the garden and watched the surgery windows for any fleeting glimpse of Sam.

Then on Thursday morning the postman came, bringing her a thick packet from India, which she opened with trembling fingers. Several letters spilled out on to her lap, two in Sam's writing and three in her grandfather's, as well as a covering note from Jim Holden to say that the clinic was doing well and Anne had settled down happily. They wished her luck in her partnership with her grandfather, and closed with a promise to visit when they were home on leave for Christmas.

She picked up her grandfather's letters and put them to one side. She wasn't sure she could cope with them at the moment. That left Sam's, and the rest of the run-of-the-mill correspondence. She made another cup of coffee, picked up all the letters and went into the sun-drenched conservatory. It was still chilly, but the sun was cheerful and she felt she needed cheering.

She ignored the electricity bill, threw

229

away a pile of junk mail from mail-order companies and the like, and with shaking fingers she opened the first letter from Sam.

CHAPTER TEN

Dear Lydia, Do you mind if I call you Lydia? Harry has talked about you so much that I feel as if I've known you for years.

I'm not sure if you have been aware of the continuing decline in your grandfather's health, but recently he has deteriorated rapidly and I thought you ought to know so that you could have an opportunity to come home and be with him. I feel that the end is probably not very far away. He has cancer of the stomach, and is no longer able to take any solids. He kicks up such a fuss when Judith and I try to feed him what he calls 'filthy slop', but it's as much as he can do to keep it down.

He needs you. He talks of you constantly, and would be so cheered to see you again. He asks daily if there is any news. I do hope you'll make the effort to come home to him. I realise that you must have responsibilities, but I feel that he ought to come first, at least in the short term. I think you must also face the fact that, as far as your grandfather is concerned, there is no other time scale.

I'm sorry to be the bearer of such bad news, but I felt you ought to know. I look forward to making you welcome when you get back. If you can phone with your travel arrangements I'll try and pick you up from the airport. Yours sincerely, Sam Davenport.

It was dated the twentieth of January. Lydia folded the letter carefully and put it down, reaching reluctantly for the second. She knew what it must contain, and she took a moment to compose herself before reading it. It was dated the third of February, and was much briefer than the first.

Dear Lydia, I am sorry to have to tell you that your grandfather died at two-thirty this morning. He was fully conscious at the time, and asked me to give you his fondest love.

Here the writing shook, and Lydia felt her eyes mist over.

She dashed away the tears and read on.

The funeral will be at the end of next week, probably on Friday afternoon. Please phone with your travel arrangements. Sincerely, Sam. PS: If it's of any comfort, it really was the hackneyed old blessed release. SD.

Picking up her coffee, she swirled it round in the cup and stared blindly down the garden. If only he had written sooner! But why hadn't Gramps told her? Why had he left her in ignorance of his illness, and yet apparently asked for her at the end?

Realising that she had the answer in her lap, she picked up her grandfather's letters and sorted them into order.

The first was dated the third of January, and was the same sort of chatty, newsy letter she had been receiving all the time. With the twenty-twenty vision of hindsight, she could see that he was skirting round the truth and softening the blow. He had probably thought he had more time.

The second was dated the eighteenth of January, and confessed that his health was in a more precarious state than he had let on.

It would be wonderful to see you again, my love. I know you must be busy, and I have tried to give you as much time as I could to get over Graham, but I fear that if you are to see me again it must be soon. I didn't want to trouble you, but I find I'm not as brave as I had thought I would be and miss my Lydia quite dreadfully. Come home, poppet. Your loving Gramps.

Her eyes clouded over and she allowed her lids to drift shut. Silly old fool, she thought fondly. She opened the third letter through the blur of tears. The writing was much more shaky, and in places was difficult to decipher. It was dated the second of February—the day before he'd died.

My darling Lydia, I have resigned myself to the fact that I will not see you again, and so while I have the chance I must explain some of my actions which may at first seem hurtful to you.

My first confession is that, as soon as I knew I would not regain my health, I informed the FHSA and recommended that Sam take over the practice. He has done an excellent job, and is a conscientious and thorough doctor, as well as a compassionate and thoroughly decent man. I know we had talked at length about your joining me in the practice, but it really is too much for one person, and I truly felt that you didn't have enough experience to handle it alone. Sam does, of course, having worked in general practice for four years now, and he was here on the spot. If I hadn't felt that the practice would overwhelm you I would have sent for you, so don't feel that by going to India you threw away your chances, because you didn't. I also wasn't sure if you had recovered from Graham's shabby treatment. Poor darling, I did ache for you, but, you know, he wasn't good enough for you.

That brings me to my second confession. I have left the practice premises to Sam, and not because he lacks the funds to purchase them or set up a surgery of his own. Indeed, with his family money he could probably buy me outright with his small change. I don't want you to feel that this is in any way a slight, or that I am favouring an intruder, although God knows no one could have been better to me than him, bless his heart. He has been a constant friend, cheerful and amusing, and yet I have been able to discuss my death with him openly and frankly. That, you know, is very valuable in coming to terms with it.

I love Sam, and would have been proud to own him as a son. I can't tell you how sorry I am that my own son was such a poor father to you. I hope that in some measure I have made up for his negligence—but I digress.

My main purpose in leaving the practice to Sam and the house to you was that it would to some extent throw you together. It has become my fondest dream that, you and Sam would become partners, both in the practice and in life itself. I could not choose a better man for you, Lydia. I hope you will forgive this intolerable interference in your life, and put it down to the harmless machinations of a feeble-minded old man. Know only that I love you, my dear, and that everything I have done I have done with your best interests at heart. Forgive me if it was all a terrible mistake. God bless you, Your loving Gramps.

Very carefully she folded the letter, put it back into the envelope and set it down on the table. Then, resting her head back against the cushions, she let the heavy, silent tears fall.

So near, and yet so far. Oh, Sam! She realised that she was crying not for her grandfather, but for herself, and for Sam, and for a broken dream.

Sam always opened the post before surgery, and scanned the letters and results quickly before the patients started to arrive. On Thursday morning he wished he hadn't done so. There was a letter from the consultant in charge of Susie Parkins. Sam read it with a heavy heart, and threw it in a drawer in the desk, to show to Lydia.

Lydia. God, how he missed her. He pressed his fingers gently against his aching eyes, and sighed. It wasn't easy always to remember that she was a scheming bitch. He saw her often, working in the garden, and she was so pale and thin now. He couldn't believe it was only ten days since he had caught her plotting with Sir James.

On impulse he opened the drawer again to take out the letter about Susie, and his eye was caught by another letter, this time from the FHSA. Frowning, he scanned it and then reread it, slowly. He gave a hollow laugh. He hadn't been wrong, then. He knew she had strings to pull, but he hadn't realised that they were that effective!

He dealt with the patients, the repeat prescriptions and the one house call, and then, picking up the two letters, he went through the house to find Lydia. She was asleep in the conservatory, curled up on Harry's favourite chair, and all around her were letters—letters from him, he noticed with a start, as well as from Harry. He looked at her closely, and realised with a sudden surge of compassion that her face was stained with tears.

He reminded himself of her perfidy, and steeled himself for an unpleasant confrontation—but not before he was armed with a cup of coffee. In another resurgence of compassion, he brought two cups.

Lydia was awoken by Sam's voice, calling her from a great distance.

'No,' she moaned, and turned her face into the cushions.

'Yes, Lydia. I want to talk to you. Wake up, please.'

She struggled to the surface, aware as she did so of her wildly untidy hair, her tear-stained face and her state of sleepy confusion, all putting her at a distinct disadvantage with the suave, well-dressed man sitting opposite her.

He didn't look that great, she decided after a second look. Worn and weary, and utterly disheartened. She didn't dare risk a third look in case she flung herself into his arms to comfort him.

Instead she picked up her coffee, tucked her feet up under her bottom and waited.

'I've had a letter from Susie's consultant,' Sam said eventually.

'And?' Her hands tightened on the cup.

'They performed a laparoscopy on Saturday, and discovered a carcinoma of the head of the pancreas, with nodal involvement. They removed it, and transferred her to intensive care, but she went into renal failure on Monday.' He

238

looked up, and Lydia's heart faltered at his expression. Defeat, humility, complete and utter despair. 'She died on Tuesday morning. I thought you'd want to know.'

'Thank you.' She realised that the coffee had spilt on to her lap and was soaking into her jeans, but she couldn't bring herself to worry about it. 'Sam, I'm so sorry. You did everything you could—'

'Did I? Damn, Lydia, I sent her away to try and put on weight—when I think of the time we wasted, testing her for this and that—'

'Sam, you aren't clairvoyant! You did the proper thing, considering the symptoms she presented you with. You can't blame yourself—'

'Can't I? You realised, at least a week before me.'

She shook her head. 'It was academic by then, anyway. We were both too slow. I just said it first. It was probably too late by the time she first came to see you.'

Slowly he nodded. 'Maybe. But I feel so helpless—what can I say to her mother?' He closed his eyes and rubbed them absently for a moment, then he looked up. 'There was another thing—a letter from the FHSA, addressed to me, lying in the desk drawer. Why didn't I get it? And why was it opened? It was marked confidential.'

'So is most of your post, Sam. It came while you were ill, and you couldn't see to read then, so I just shoved it in the drawer and forgot about it. I meant to take it away again.'

'How dare you intercept my mail?'

Sudden hot tears flooded her eyes. 'Shut up, Sam,' she said quietly. 'I meant to write to them and ask them if they would mind rewording the letter, leaving out the reference to me. I didn't want you seeing it like that and thinking the worst.'

'What worst? That you were after a partnership in the practice any way you could get it? Tell me something—did you have to sleep with Sir James?'

'You are contemptible,' she whispered, her heart breaking. 'Thank God my grandfather never knew what a viper he was nursing in his breast. I didn't want you thinking that I had anything to do with the recommendations for another partner, especially not me. I swear, I knew nothing about that letter or what prompted it. I already knew how you felt about women doctors, and I knew after you overheard me talking to Sir James that you would misconstrue anything you could to prove I was just another bitch like the others you'd got yourself mixed up with; that way you could get yourself neatly off the hook without taking any responsibility. You're just too scared to make a commitment, aren't you, Sam? Here—' she thrust her grandfather's last and longest letter at him '—read this. See what the poor fool thought of you.'

He read it in silence, and when he had finished he put it down on the table and stared at his hands for several minutes without a sound.

When he did speak his voice was strangely expressionless.

'Who was Graham?'

'Graham?' She was startled. Whatever she had expected, it wasn't that. 'He—we were going out together, before I went to India. He's a doctor—a plastic surgeon, strangely enough. I—just couldn't be what he wanted me to be.'

'Faithful?' Sam said harshly, but she could see it hurt him to say the word. She ignored him and continued.

'He wanted me to sleep with him. I refused. Eventually he got fed up with waiting. I found him in bed with my flatmate.'

'Oh, my God. I'm sorry. That must have been horrific.'

'Just a blow to my pride, really—that and my ego. I wasn't really hurt—he didn't have the power to hurt me.' Unlike you, she finished in her head.

'Why couldn't you talk to me about joining me in the practice? Why go to Sir James, and go to all these lengths to make yourself "indispensable" to me—why not be honest?'

'I didn't go to Sir James—'

'Lydia, I *heard* you—'

'No! No, Sam, you *thought* you heard me. There's a difference. He was asking about your health, following your accident.'

'What about all the mistakes I was supposed to have made?' Sam's voice was brittle with anger.

'Falling over the end of the bed, dropping the blanket in the fire—those sorts of mistakes. Insisting on having the bath. Things like that. And as for talk of partnership, we were talking about love, Sam. Our love—yours and mine. We had just spent that idyllic weekend—it was only fair to assume, I thought, that all the talk of love should mean something. We have to trust, you said—well, I did, Sam, but you couldn't, could you? You couldn't trust me, you never did believe in me, and now it's too late. You've convinced yourself that I'm a liar and a cheat, and a whore to boot—shall I tell you something funny, Sam? I saved myself for twenty-nine years—and when I gave you my virginity you didn't even realise. Isn't that the sickest thing you ever heard?'

After a long pause he raised his eyes to hers, and the raw agony in them made her want to weep for him. 'I don't know what to say,' he confessed.

'Tough. I'm sick of telling you how to apologise to me, Sam. I'd like to be alone now.'

He stood and made his way towards the door, but she stopped him.

'Here,' she thrust the letter about Susie at him, 'you'll need this to close her file.'

He took it wordlessly, but as he turned Lydia saw the tears well in his eyes—whether for her or for Susie, she didn't know. Either way, it was too late.

She found a note on the mat on Friday morning.

'Susie's funeral is at two. Her mother has asked us to attend—will you come, please?'

She wore a grey jersey dress which clung provocatively but, when covered by her black wool coat, struck just the right note. Sam was waiting for her at a quarter to two, and they walked down to the church together in silence and made their way to a pew at the back.

'I feel I have no right to be here,' Sam muttered.

Lydia squeezed his hand unobtrusively, and shifted a little closer to him. He was taking this very personally, and she was worried about him. She would have thought he was too professional to get so involved, but obviously she was wrong. He took his mission of saving life very seriously, and couldn't cope with the prospect of defeat—especially not this defeat. His grip on her hand was nothing short of painful.

The service was short, simple and very beautiful. The church was smothered in spring flowers, and the whole feeling was one of sunshine.

Sam was unable to sing. He stood in silence, deep in thought, and Lydia ached for him.

They didn't go to the graveside, standing instead by the church to give the family privacy, but Mrs Parkins broke away from the group and came up to them as they were leaving. Her face was pale and her eyes were red-rimmed, but she was calm and composed.

'I wanted to thank you,' she said. 'I realise that there was nothing anyone could have done, but you both tried so hard for her.'

'I'm sorry we failed,' Sam said heavily.

'You didn't fail,' Mrs Parkins responded quietly. 'You took away her fear. I can never thank you enough for that.'

She rejoined the others then, and Sam and Lydia made their way back up the hill to the house.

'Coffee?' Lydia suggested, but Sam shook his head.

'I've got a clinic in about half an hour, and I—frankly, I want to be on my own. Do you mind?'

'No. You go ahead. I'll be here if you need me.'

He gave her a searching, agonised look,

and then turned briskly away and strode into the surgery.

Lydia made her way into the house and put the kettle on for a cup of tea, then took it into the sitting-room. The sun was pouring in, and it looked lovely with the new decorations.

The hall was greatly improved as well, only the kitchen now letting down the house. Well, she could get that refitted if necessary.

With a heavy sigh, she picked up the phone.

There was a knock on the door at seven. She opened it to Sam, who was standing in the porch looking devastatingly attractive. He was freshly showered, and wearing pleated fawn twill trousers and a soft green shirt that was almost exactly the colour of his eyes. He had a brown paper bag in one hand and a huge bunch of flowers in the other, and he looked thoroughly nervous.

She didn't know exactly what to say to him, so she held the door open and let him in.

'Have you eaten?' he asked in a strained voice.

'No. I couldn't be bothered.'

'Oh. I got a Chinese takeaway delivered. I forgot—' he thrust the flowers at her '—these are for you.'

'Say it with flowers,' she murmured. 'What are you saying, Sam? Another apology?'

He looked at his feet, and then raised his eyes to hers with a helpless sigh. 'I'm sorry. I've behaved like a heel.'

She smiled slightly. 'Ten out of ten. Shall we eat? I've got something to tell you.'

She went into the kitchen and shoved the flowers ruthlessly into a bowl of cold water in the sink, and then opened a cupboard.

'I've laid the table upstairs in my flat,' Sam said, not altogether happily. Things were not going according to his plan, obviously.

'Fine,' she replied, and hoped to God it would be. His nearness was doing crazy things to her heart, but she dared not give in to instinct and throw herself in his arms. She simply couldn't stand the pain when he opened them again and dropped her.

He followed her up the stairs and through the communicating door, and then cannoned into her back as she came to a dead halt.

The table had been pulled out into the room, and was laid with a gleaming white cloth and sparkling crystal. There were finger-bowls with petals floating in the water, and here and there low lamps shed soft pools of light on the floor. A single candle flickered in the middle of the table.

She was speechless while Sam, visibly nervous, removed the warm plates from the oven and set out the dishes on the table.

He held her chair for her, and then flapped solicitously around, arranging her napkin and pouring the wine.

'Sam, what's going on?' she asked at last.

'Ah,' he said heavily. 'You first. You said you had something to tell me.'

She toyed with her food for a moment, and then pushed the plate away. 'I've decided to put the house on the market,' she said eventually.

'Oh.'

'Just "oh"? Nothing about capitalising on my inheritance?'

'Don't—'

'Sorry. Anyway, the agent came this

248

afternoon and made all sorts of noises. He's coming back tomorrow to take some photos. It will give me the capital to buy into a practice somewhere—I may as well. There's nothing for me here. The estate agent was a bit concerned about access, though. We'll have to sort out the problem of the drive.' She met his bleak look with one of her own. 'Your turn now.'

'There won't be a problem with the drive. I'm giving the practice back to you.'

'Why? How can you? That's silly—'

'As you know, the FHSA want George and me to set up a health centre, in a purpose-built surgery in one of the villages. There are a couple of potential sites. When that happens I won't need the surgery. I thought I'd buy a house in the village and use the sitting-room just for a weekly surgery for those who can't travel.'

'Why don't you buy this off me, then? Gramps reckoned you were filthy rich enough—why not? Then you can carry on here until the health centre's built. You'd have room here then for the other partner, too.'

There was a huge lump in her throat, and she could hardly speak round it.

'Lydia, that was why I wanted to talk to you. First of all to apologise for the way I've treated you right from the beginning. You've done nothing to give me any reason to doubt or mistrust you, but I've managed to find things or make them up. You were wrong about me—I don't want to avoid commitment. I was coming to find you to tell you I'd got my hearing back and ask you to marry me, when I heard you talking to Sir James. I wanted to wait until I could hear you say yes. Instead, I heard you say you were working on our partnership! That's why I went so wild.

'I couldn't believe it. The things I'd felt with you I'd never felt before. I thought I loved Jo, but it was just calf-love—hero-worship, even. Sarah and I—well, we were good friends, but we didn't have enough to last a lifetime. I got over them both fairly quickly. But you—I'll never get over you, Lydia. You've got my soul.'

He was staring into his wine glass, his eyes hidden, but then suddenly he looked up at her and she saw his heart laid bare.

'That was why I was so hurt. I couldn't believe that something so wonderful to me could be just a means to an end for you.

250

I just lashed out—I wanted to hurt you as much as you were hurting me.' He paused, as if he was struggling to find the words. 'I know I have no right to ask or expect it of you, but I need your forgiveness. I love you, and I want to be with you forever. Life's too short— I realised that today, at Susie's funeral. All through it I kept thinking that it could have been you—that if I let you go I won't be there for you when you need me. You'll have someone else's children, lie in someone else's arms—' his voice cracked, but he carried on '—I can't let that happen, if there's the slightest chance for us.

'I will buy the house from you—but only if you'll let me give it to you as a wedding present. You belong here, with me—with our children. I can't stay here without you. I'd see you everywhere, in every nook and cranny—darling, talk to me...'

His voice cracked again, and she reached out her hand blindly to him.

'Sam—'

Suddenly she was in his arms, crushed hard against his chest as he hung on for dear life, and then his mouth found hers, clinging to her in desperation. After a few seconds it gentled, soothing and caressing, and then the heat seared between them and they were lost. She was aware of Sam lifting her and carrying her through to the bedroom, then the world receded, leaving them alone together in the cleansing flames.

Much later Lydia drew the tip of her finger down Sam's nose and then traced the line of his lips, curved in a self-satisfied smile.

'Of course,' she murmured, her voice husky in the aftermath of passion, 'I'll want a good price for the house.'

Sam laughed weakly. 'I expected nothing less. You'll need the money anyway.'

'Why?'

He propped himself up on one elbow and looked down into her eyes. 'I've been talking to George. We want you to come into the practice with us. It wouldn't work if it was just the two of us, you and me, because we'd never have a weekend together, but with the three of us we should be able to arrange it to everyone's satisfaction.'

'You were very confident,' she said drily, a slight smile playing about the corners of her mouth, but his face was serious.

'I was fighting for my life. I don't know what I would have done if you'd said no.'

She swallowed. 'I can't say no to you, Sam. We're in the same predicament. I've given you my soul.'

His face softened with regret. 'I'm sorry I hurt you.'

'You're getting good at that, aren't you?' she teased. 'I think we'll have a little ceremony every morning, just to keep you in order—'

'Don't push your luck,' he threatened laughingly. His head lowered until his lips were brushing hers. 'Anyway, what's all this about not being able to say no to me...?'

'Mmm. You're getting good at that, too.'

'Flatterer.'

He kissed her again. 'OK?'

'Mmm. There's always room for improvement.'

'We'll have to have a little ceremony every morning, just to keep me in order,' he said with a low laugh. 'After all, practice makes perfect...'

The publishers hope that this book has given you enjoyable reading. Large Print Books are especially designed to be as easy to see and hold as possible. If you wish a complete list of our books, please ask at your local library or write directly to: Dales Large Print Books, Long Preston, North Yorkshire, BD23 4ND, England.

This Large Print Book for the Partially sighted, who cannot read normal print, is published under the auspices of

THE ULVERSCROFT FOUNDATION